Unidentified Suburban Object

MIKE JUNG

SCHOLASTIC INC.

Copyright © 2016 by Mike Jung

Arthur A. Levine Books hardcover edition designed by Carol Ly, published by Arthur A. Levine Books, an imprint of Scholastic Inc., May 2016.

All rights reserved. Published by Scholastic Inc., *Publishers since 1920*. SCHOLASTIC, the LANTERN LOGO, and associated logos are trademarks and/or registered trademarks of Scholastic Inc.

The publisher does not have any control over and does not assume any responsibility for author or third-party websites or their content.

No part of this publication may be reproduced, stored in a retrieval system, or transmitted in any form or by any means, electronic, mechanical, photocopying, recording, or otherwise, without written permission of the publisher. For information regarding permission, write to Scholastic Inc., Attention: Permissions Department, 557 Broadway, New York, NY 10012.

ISBN 978-0-545-78227-2

10 9 8 7 6 5 4 3 2   17 18 19 20 21

Printed in the U.S.A.   40

First printing 2017

Book design by Carol Ly

FOR ELLEN OH AND MARTHA WHITE,
BECAUSE FRIENDS AND CRITIQUE PARTNERS
WHO CAN MERCILESSLY HOLD MY CREATIVE FEET
TO THE FIRE WHILE ALSO MAKING ME THINK
"AW, THEY'RE SO SMART AND FUNNY WHEN
THEY INCINERATE MY FEET LIKE THIS" TOTALLY
DESERVE TO HAVE A BOOK DEDICATED TO THEM.

ONE

THE RECIPE FOR KOREAN DUMPLINGS ON THE
K-Chow Goddess's blog has a picture of her dumplings after they've been made but before they've been
cooked, and they look so good you can practically
smell them. The filling is exactly in the middle of the
dumpling; the crinkles in the wrapper are evenly
spaced and totally identical; and each finished dumpling looks like it could be hanging from somebody's
earlobe if it was 10 percent of its original size.

Yes, I'm good at math. All Koreans are, didn't you
know? Yes, I'm good at sarcasm too.

Shelley and I crossed our arms, shoulders touching,
and stared at a printout of the recipe, which lay on
the table in front of our own platter of newly made
dumplings.

"Our dumplings," I finally said, "do not look like
her dumplings."

"I'm not sure what they do look like." Shelley

scratched her nose, leaving a small streak of soy sauce and sesame oil. "Baby squirrels?"

"Mutant baby squirrels is more like it." I picked up a dumpling and poked at its edge. You're supposed to fold the round pastry wrappers in half with a lump of filling in the middle and seal the edges together with a little bit of water. Our edges kept springing leaks.

"Mandu, right?" Shelley said.

"Is that what these are? I'm not so sure."

"They'll probably still taste good," Shelley said in a firm voice, which I totally knew she was going to say. Best friends are predictable like that.

"Oh yeah, mutant baby squirrels are always delicious."

"Today on *Survival of the Weirdest*, watch as new cast member Chloe eats a mutant baby squirrel!"

"I could totally have my own reality show. Okay, I guess we need to fry the baby squirrels now."

"Oh sure, let's absolutely add some burning hot oil to the mix." Shelley snorted as I started pouring vegetable oil into my dad's big frying pan.

The frying process was . . . exciting.

"Flip them! You have to flip them!" I shouted over the sizzling of hot oil, making a shoveling motion with one hand. The dumplings we'd put into the pan were ugly, but at least each of them had been in one piece. That wasn't true anymore.

"What do you think I'm trying to do? They're sticking to the pan!" Shelley shouted back. She held the handle of the pan with an oven mitt and scraped at the dumplings with short, choppy motions. A thin haze of smoke drifted through the kitchen.

"Hold on, I'm gonna put in more oil!"

Shelley leaned back as I tilted the oil bottle over the pan. I tried to pour the oil slowly and evenly, but when it hit the pan it made a huge sizzle and sprayed up in the air like liquid death. Shelley let go of the pan as we screamed and jumped back from the stove. The smoke got a little thicker.

"That didn't work," I said.

"Yeah, oops." Shelley waved at the smoke with her oven-mittened hand.

I put on the oven mitt Shelley wasn't wearing, moved the pan to an unlit burner, and turned off the lit burner. The pan was still spitting oil and I didn't feel like deep-frying my face, so I had to stretch my arm out as far as possible. I stepped back as Shelley reached up and turned on the fan over the stove.

"Cooking mandu is hard." I thought Shelley's pronunciation of "mandu" was better than mine, even though we learned it from the same YouTube video.

"Yeah. Loud too. Do you think they're done?"

Shelley snorted again. She pulled a big plate out of the dish drainer and held it while I scraped the dumplings out of the pan.

"They don't actually look that bad," I said. "I'd eat that one piece right there, the one with . . . oh wait, I didn't see that. It's complete charcoal on the other side."

"No, look, there's a whole . . . huh." Shelley's shoulders sagged a little bit. "Never mind. Geez, the edges of the wrappers don't stick together at all, do they?"

"We're probably doing it wrong. But look, the filling from this one held its shape!" I held up the spatula, which had an oval lump of cooked meat and vegetables balanced on it.

A few minutes later the first platter of fried mandu was on the kitchen table.

"Okay, so here's what we do." I scooped a pile of dumpling fragments onto Shelley's plate. "We just pretend they're all in one piece."

"Oh, that's a genius plan."

"Foolproof."

"Hey, they're okay!" Shelley said around a mouthful of dumpling bits and pieces.

I nodded, chewing, then swallowed. "You have to make sure you get some of the wrapper mixed up with the filling, though. The filling's kind of mushy by itself."

"How do you think—" Shelley was interrupted by the sound of a key turning in the front door.

"Helloooooo," Dad said as he closed the door behind him. "Wow, something smells good."

"You want to try some, Dad?" I used my fork to stab a dumpling that wasn't completely falling apart and bounced up from my chair as Dad covered the six steps between the front door and the kitchen. His face had that crinkly forehead expression it gets after a really busy day at work, but he smiled when he saw me holding up the fork.

"What's this?" Dad said, giving me a kiss on the top of the head and looking at the mangled dumpling. He wore a white shirt, beige cargo pants, and leather sandals—he runs an aquarium store, so it's not like he needs to wear a tuxedo to work.

"Mandu," I said cheerfully.

Dad looked at me with a blank expression, as if he didn't know what I was talking about.

". . . Uh, Dad? You know, Korean dumplings?"

"Oh, *mandu*!" Dad's eyebrows shot up like a couple

of tiny, startled birds. "Yes, right, dumplings." He put his leather satchel down on the kitchen table and scratched his scalp, making a big clump of his hair stand up.

"I haven't had . . . mandu in a long time." Dad's pronunciation of "mandu" was more like mine than like Shelley's. "Where did you get the recipe?" Dad took the fork from me and held the dumpling up, inspecting it like it was a diamond.

"*The K-Chow Goddess.*" Shelley smiled a big toothy smile at Dad, who smiled back. "It's a food blog."

"Was this your idea, Shelley?"

"No, it was mine," I said. Why was he asking Shelley that question?

Dad smiled at me, but it was a more complicated smile than the one he gave Shelley. It was more, I don't know, droopy in the eyes, maybe even sad. He kissed me on the head again, and we sat down at the table.

"Mandu." The way Dad said it you'd think he was saying "Atlantis" or "Bigfoot" — like he could hardly believe he was looking at something real. He took a bite and chewed slowly, with a very spaced-out look on his face.

"Um, Dad . . ." I said after what felt like a couple of minutes had gone by. "What do you think? Good?"

Dad smiled, but it was one of those mouth-only smiles.

"Good," he said. "Just like your grandmother used to make."

I looked at Shelley out of the corner of my eye. I could tell she was trying to control her face, but her eyes were so wide open that it looked like her forehead was being pushed closer to the top of her head.

"Your mom's mandu was just like this, Mr. Cho?" Shelley said.

"Yes, it was," Dad said, but he was totally lying. After almost thirteen years of having him as my dad, I could tell. Ow. There was suddenly a lump in my throat, and I clamped my lips together and swallowed hard.

"You know what, girls, I have some work to do." Dad got up and slung his bag over his shoulder, then ran a hand over his head, which kind of smoothed out his hair but not really.

He eyeballed the kitchen table and the counters, which were covered with cooking stuff, bowls, cutting boards, and assorted vegetable scraps. "You really went to a lot of trouble to make these, didn't you?"

"Yup," Shelley said. Dad chuckled as he picked up an empty can.

"Canned mung bean sprouts. They actually have these at Speedwell's?"

"No," I said. "We ordered a bunch of stuff from the Internet."

I must have sounded at least a little mad, because Dad stopped chuckling and looked at me with his head tilted forward.

"Chloe? Are you okay?"

"Fine," I said, drawing out the "F" and biting off the end of the word.

"Are you sure?"

Clueless dads are the worst, aren't they? I let out a gusty lungful of air and smiled at him, sort of. He smiled back and kissed the top of my head again.

He started walking toward the master bedroom but paused in mid-step, turned around, and came back to the table. He gave me a *fourth* kiss on the head (Dad likes kissing people on the head, obviously), then headed back to his and Mom's bedroom.

Shelley and I sat there for a minute, the mandu forgotten on the table in front of us.

"So . . ." Shelley said. "That was strange, right?"

"Yeah, that was." I chewed on the edge of my thumbnail for a second.

"Your dad does actually know what mandu is, right?"

"Duh, yeah. He was born in Korea and everything."

I forked up some dumpling bits and slowly started chewing them. "You know what's weird?"

"I know a lot of things that are weird, but I don't know which one you're talking about right now."

I swallowed hard and got up to get a glass of water. "Come on, Shelley, you've only been over here every single day since forever." I walked around the table, slipped behind Shelley's chair, and went to the kitchen sink. "Have you ever heard my mom and dad talk about that stuff?"

"About what stuff?" Shelley grabbed the half-empty platter of mandu and put it on the counter between the kitchen and dining room. "You mean being Korean?"

"Yeah. Being Korean." I took a long drink of water, wiped my mouth on my sleeve, and leaned my back against the edge of the kitchen sink.

"They never talk about it, right? Don't you think that's weird?"

"I don't know. It's not like my parents talk about being from England."

"Maybe, but they weren't born there, were they? My parents are *from* Korea but they still never talk about it."

"They sound American. Well, mostly."

"Duh, they know English."

"I mean they don't have really thick accents or anything. Just a little."

"They've been here a long time. It's . . . I don't know, it's just bizarre."

"I guess. We're keeping these, right?" Shelley held up the platter of uncooked dumplings—we'd only cooked about a quarter of the whole amount. "This is two weeks of babysitting money right here."

"Yeah, let's freeze 'em."

After cleaning up, we went to my room to finish the process of getting ready for school.

It was a miracle that Mom and Dad finally let me start buying clothes online—they were sure I'd accidentally buy a pickup truck or something—but it took seven years of in-store shopping (which included three years of in-store fighting) to get there. Shelley must have been thinking the same thing.

"I can't believe you can finally pick your own clothes!"

"Well, I can't always—Mom and Dad shot down a few things. I don't have to go to Wallingford's any-more, though." I shuddered. "Hey, want to see what I found in the back of my closet last night?"

"Totally—is it what I think it is?"

"Probably." I walked to the closet, went digging in one of the plastic boxes on the floor, and emerged with a football jersey.

"Oh wow," Shelley said, snorting with laughter. "A Condors jersey. EVERYONE was wearing those things."

"So ugly," I said, shaking my head.

The Capital City Condors were the best team in football during fourth grade, so of course everyone in Primrose Heights turned into a fashion lemming and HAD to have a Condors shirt of some kind.

Yeah, I turned into a lemming too.

"Shopping for this thing was the worst," I said. "I was surprised they didn't demolish Wallingford's and rebuild it in the shape of a football."

"I still can't believe you wore that all year," Shelley said, holding out her hands. I tossed the horrible jersey to her.

"Yeah, well, you had one too."

"I had three, and unlike you, I actually liked them."

Shelley was right—I'd never actually liked that hideous jersey. That wasn't the point, of course—the point was to *fit in, yeah, go, Condors!*

"Mom was soooooo into it," I said.

I could still see how her face had looked when I pulled a Condors jersey off the shelf—a huge, open-mouthed, OMG-style smile. She practically vomited happiness. Football jerseys! If fashion police actually existed we'd have all gone to jail for the rest of our lives. My clothes sure looked like everyone else's, though.

In fifth grade I decided it'd be nice to wear clothes I actually liked, because superstripey maxi dresses were what all the annoying girls wore and that is just not the look for non-toothpick-shaped Chloe Cho. So I started my campaign to pick my own school clothes, and after proving I could earn my own money (by babysitting and working at the fish store), buy clothes online without accidentally applying to college, and return stuff that didn't fit right without whining, I finally got to shop for clothes online. It only took THREE YEARS.

"I can't believe tomorrow's finally the first day of school," Shelley said as I held up the skirt I'd ordered through ThriftStoreBetty.com the week before. "I like that one."

"Thanks, and I know, finally! Look, this was a total steal." I put on my new vintage jacket, the one with the pattern of tiny red flowers all over the sleeves, and spun around with my arms extended.

"I couldn't wear that, but it looks good on you."

"You brought your stuff, right?" I shrugged off the jacket.

"Yeah. Not the books, but everything else." Shelley hoisted her backpack off the floor and onto my bed while I pulled a plastic box of school supplies out from under the bed.

We spent a totally awesome hour analyzing notebook designs, organizing markers and pencils, and deciding what buttons to pin on our backpacks before we got around to comparing our class schedules.

I groaned. "So we only have three classes together? That sucks."

"Yeah, but did you see this one?" Shelley pointed at the grid of classes on her schedule. "Social studies with Ms. Lee."

"I saw that! There's no Lee family in Primrose Heights; she must be from out of town. Wild."

Shelley grinned her crafty, sideways, I-know-something-you-don't grin.

"Oh, it's even wilder than that," she said. "My dad went to the school board meeting last night—her whole name's Su-Hyung Lee."

Whoa.

"Seriously?"

"Seriously. I think that might mean she's . . ."

"Asian." My mind was blown. All of the teachers I'd ever had in my entire life were white. Every single one of them.

"Yeah, and you know the thing about people with the last names Park, Kim, or Lee. She must be—"

"*Korean!*"

TWO

Mom's the kind of cook who could burn water, so it wasn't a big shock when she came home from work with a bag of takeout.

"Fingerlickin' Chicken again?" Dad said as we pulled our chairs up to the Korean-food-free dining room table. I looked down so Mom wouldn't see me grinning, but she did anyway.

"Look, you've turned our daughter against me again," Mom said, but she smiled and reached out to touch my hair. "I can't help it if she's getting better at cooking than me."

"Getting?" I said. Mom, still smiling, flapped her hand at me like she was waving away a mosquito.

"Oh, I like fried chicken, but three times a week is a bit much." Dad gave me one of his arched-eyebrow looks, which doesn't look nearly as funny as he thinks it does, as he took a bite out of a drumstick.

"I saw all the bowls and pans in the dishwasher,"

Mom said with a smile. "So . . . what did you make this time?"

"Mandu," I said. I sat up a little straighter, crossed arms on the table, and looked at Mom with a fake casual expression on my face.

The first time I tried to make Korean food Mom's eyes got all buggy, and she immediately got into a loud-whisper conversation with Dad when I pushed two bowls of bibimbap in front of them.

You know what's awful? Making a surprise Korean dinner for your parents and watching them push it around on their plates until one of them says she's actually in the mood for pizza. You'd think they'd just pretend to like something their only kid cooked for them, but oh no.

"Mandu? Really." Mom didn't exactly stop smiling, but her smile did get a little frozen-looking. "Where'd you get the recipe?"

"*The K-Chow Goddess*," I said, still looking Mom straight in the eye.

"It's a cooking blog," Dad said.

Somehow I was always surprised by how tech-savvy Dad is. He talks and acts like this very mellow Zen master person who only likes fish and trees and stuff like that, but he knows way more about the Internet than Mom.

I guess my traitor face gave me away again, because Dad laughed in that way of his, where it's more like he's hissing softly.

"You always look so surprised when I talk about the Internet," he said, reaching over and brushing a few stray hairs back from my forehead. I blew at his fingers as he pulled them away from my head.

"I know about the K-Chow Goddess too." Mom tapped Dad's chin with her fingernails. He reached up with one hand, palm turned toward his face, and gently clasped his fingers with hers. Blech, but I wasn't fooled: Mom was about to change the subject. Three . . . two . . . one . . .

"Are you all ready for tomorrow?" she said. "We can make a last-minute trip to Wallingford's tonight, if you need to."

"Wallingford's, also known as The House of Conformity? Thanks, Mom, but no thanks. I wish there was a real thrift store in this stupid town."

"That would be nice, wouldn't it?"

"Do you know how to make mandu, Mom?"

Mom burst out laughing.

"Me?" Her shoulders hitched up and down, and she rested one hand on her forehead.

"Didn't your mom teach you? Isn't that what they did back in, you know, the old country?"

Mom got up from the table, bent over me from behind my chair, and kissed me on the top of my head, which I knew meant she was about to ignore my question.

"Honey, you know I'm not very good in the kitchen—I'm an astrophysicist, not a chef. Your dad probably wishes he married someone else twenty times a day."

"Not even once," Dad said as he started clearing the table.

"But you must have—"

"No, sweetheart, I'm as American as you are."

"Can you answer my question?" I barked. Mom leaned the top half of her body away from me.

"Hey, hey," Mom said. "You don't need to raise your voice."

"I'M NOT RAISING MY VOICE," I said. "Shelley's parents actually like it when she asks questions about her family, but with you guys it's like banging my face against a wall."

Mom and Dad looked at each other with their crinkly eyebrow, Chloe's-on-a-rampage faces, which always makes me want to chew on a rock.

"Oh, forget it," I said. "I'll be in my room."

"Dishes in the sink," Mom said. Smiling! Why was she still smiling?

"Yeah, yeah." I stomped into the kitchen and put my plate and glass into the sink, instead of giving in to my urge to hold them a foot above the sink and let them drop.

I didn't have any rocks in my room to chew on, so I split my time evenly between reorganizing my school supplies, trying on a few different combinations of stuff for my first-day-of-school outfit, and wondering if this year would be any different from every other year. After deciding to stick with the outfit I'd shown Shelley, I flopped down in my chair, slumped down on my desk, and stared at my ball python, Kaa, in his tank on the desktop. He looked a little depressed in there.

"I know how you feel," I said.

According to Dad, who has a bookshelf in the living room completely filled with books about fish, Primrose Heights is a really good habitat for koi. It's not too hot or cold, and there are enough trees to provide shade but not enough to make it like a forest. So yeah, that's why we live in this tiny, middle-of-nowhere, whiter-than-white-bread town. Because it means my dad can have a pond full of goldfish in the backyard. It's a special kind of koi that he breeds himself, but still. They're big goldfish.

I dug my schedule out of the folder of school papers

in my backpack and held it in front of my nose, looking at the list of teachers one more time.

Su-Hyung Lee. Was she Korean? Maybe I could talk to her about the stuff my parents always blew off. Maybe things actually would be different this year.

THREE

I WAS REALLY HOPING THE FIRST DAY OF SEVENTH grade wouldn't end up being the best day of the whole school year like it was in fifth grade — breaking your arm on the second day of school, combined with the worst homeroom teacher ever, will do that.

"Chloe Cho-ee," Ms. Borland called during the first, pre-broken-arm day of fifth grade. It wasn't the first time a teacher had totally put me in the spotlight because of my name, but the idiotic rhyming thing was new.

"It's Cho," I said, quietly but loudly enough to be heard.

"Oh, I know, I'm just having a little fun with you!" Ms. Borland did a little ha-ha-I'm-so-funny laugh, which was funny because she was so not funny.

"It's not Cho-ee," I muttered.

She did it on the second day of school too. The only reason she didn't do it on the third day of school was because Chase Edwards blew through a stop sign on his skateboard and made me crash my bike, land on the curb arm-first, go to the hospital, and miss the third day.

That was the past, though, and I felt optimistic as I walked through the front doors with the rest of the new seventh graders. It was a new year, my biggest enemy on the soccer team had moved away, and there was a new teacher with a Korean-sounding name who was probably guaranteed to not make fun of my last name. It was already the most interesting first day of school ever.

It wasn't like having a maybe-Korean teacher in school was ALL good, though.

"Hey, Chloe, do you know the new teacher?" a girl said right after the third-period bell rang.

Shelley and I walked through the halls with the rest of the seventh graders (everyone who wasn't going to the bathroom, comparing outfits, or super-intensely texting each other, anyway) and headed for social studies.

Predictably, it was Lindsay Crisp. Lindsay doesn't bother me that much, even if she's not exactly the sharpest knife in the drawer, so I tried not to sound too annoyed. I probably sounded annoyed anyway.

"Why would I?"

The thing about Lindsay that's both horrible and awesome is how she'll just say whatever she's really thinking, no matter how annoyed the person she's talking to might be.

"Well, you know. My mom says the new teacher's Korean, and . . ." Lindsay trailed off as I stared at her.

"Yeah, Chloe, don't all you Korean people know each other?" Shelley said it with a totally straight face, which is one of her greatest talents.

"We do, actually," I said, totally deadpan. "We hang out at all the same places and stuff."

"Yeah, I thought . . . wait, are you making fun of me?" Lindsay's hazel eyes (I was totally jealous of her eye color) suddenly drooped down at the corners. I felt a little pang of guilt.

"We're just kidding around, Lindsay."

"I didn't mean . . . I just thought you might know her, that's all." Lindsay's expression made her look like a ponytailed puppy dog.

"I don't."

Oops, there was Angry Chloe again. Sigh . . .

"I'm sorry, Chloe, geez! You're such a Crabby McCrabberson!"

"I . . . just forget it, Lindsay. *I'm* sorry, okay?"

Sheesh. The thing is, I'm the *only* Asian kid in the whole school. In the whole town, actually. Rumor has it a bunch of Japanese kids flew over the town in an airplane once, but other than that it's just me, waving my freak flag solo.

"Did she seriously call you Crabby McCrabberson?" Shelley said under her breath as Lindsay walked off in a huff.

"Yeah, that's a new one. Chloe Crabby McCrabberson Cho. Lots of C's in that name . . ."

"Su-Hyung Lee's a pretty name," Shelley said as everybody lined up at the door to room 117, which was still closed.

"It's definitely prettier than Crabby McCrabberson." We cracked up.

The door opened, and Shelley and I looked up to see the mysterious Ms. Lee in the doorway.

Ms. Lee looked a lot like any other teacher, with the exception of definitely being Asian. She wore a white, buttoned shirt (nicer and more tailored than the ones my dad always wore) and a black skirt that ended a couple of inches above the knee. She had superglossy black hair that fell around her face in a pageboy cut, and earrings with some kind of light green stone in them. She looked younger than any of our other teachers—she almost looked like a teenager, in fact. If she wasn't a teacher, I might have thought she was in high school.

It was really strange to see an Asian adult who wasn't my mom or dad.

"You must be Chloe," Ms. Lee said with a smile. She tucked a strand of hair behind her ear with a quick, precise motion.

"Uhhh . . ." I said. I closed my mouth with a snap. "Uh, I mean, yes, I'm Chloe."

"Come on in."

Ms. Lee opened the door all the way and walked into the classroom. The rest of the class was in line behind me and Shelley, and there was a lot of whispering as we filed into the room.

"Is that our new social studies teacher?" "What happened to Mr. Dowling?" "Is she Chinese or Japanese?"

Oh for crying out loud, like Chinese and Japanese were the only choices. Idiots.

Shelley grabbed me by the elbow as we took our usual seats—the front row, halfway between the windows on our left and the center of the room. Ms. Lee was writing her name on the chalkboard, and as she turned to face the class a beam of sunlight came through the windows and hit her, casting her shadow on the wall behind her.

"Good morning, class. Who can explain the relationship between a primary source document and a secondary source document?"

Dead silence. Huh?

Ms. Lee smiled, twisting up the right side of her mouth.

"Okay then, who can tell me the best method for understanding the historical context of a research topic?"

Holy cow. Was this what the class was going to be like? One of those really HARD classes? Awesome.

Bring it, I thought.

"Anyone?" Ms. Lee crossed her arms and slowly scanned the whole room, tilting her head just a little bit to the side in an oh-come-on way. I looked at Shelley, who had a big grin on her face. I caught her eye and silently mouthed "Teacher's pet" at her. She flicked her eyes at Ms. Lee and made a very subtle wing-flapping motion with her elbows.

Was she calling me a chicken? Oh no. No WAY was I letting her get away with that. I raised my hand, and Ms. Lee immediately pointed at me.

"Chloe!"

Rule number one about asking questions in class:

Teachers love students who take chances, like answering a question when everyone else in the class looks like they're about to hide under their desks.

"Reading," I said. I was totally guessing, but I'm a good guesser. "The best way to understand a topic's historical context is reading books about it."

Ms. Lee smiled. It was a good smile, lots of teeth, very cheerful-looking.

"Yes! Very good! To be more precise, you should read background material — books on related topics during the same historical period. That's a taste of what we're going to explore in the first quarter of this year: how to do historical research."

I looked sideways at Shelley and waggled my eyebrows. Shelley twirled her index finger in the air. Ms. Lee started walking back and forth at the front of the classroom, pointing her toes like a ballet dancer for just an extra half second in the middle of each step.

"My name is Ms. Lee, and as you've no doubt already noticed, I'm new to George Matthew K through 8 School. Last week the school gave me a box full of your files, which I've read, so I know you're a quality group of students who've been together a long time. I also think you're ready to take a big step forward with your studies, particularly in social studies."

There were some very quiet mutters around the

room when she said that part—kids were definitely worried Ms. Lee was a hard teacher. Slackers.

"I'm going to show you how global history and personal history aren't separate things, but always connected, whether your ancestry is German, Venezuelan, or Korean."

Ms. Lee passed by my desk as she said "Korean," and she didn't look at me or wink or anything like that, but she did put her hand on my desk for just a second, and when she took it away there was a small, folded piece of paper there.

Was that a *note*? I quickly slid my own hand over it, and as Ms. Lee turned away from my desk I shot a look at Shelley. Her mouth was actually hanging open, and I was sure she was thinking the same thing I was:

A note from a teacher?

Ms. Lee stopped pacing and stood in the center of the room with her arms crossed and one hip stuck out to the side.

"We're going to work hard in this class, and I do mean *we*. History is partly about achievements that force people to remember you, and that's the standard we're going to strive for. I want you to remember me—hopefully because I've made you learn and think about history in a new way. And I want to remember you for what you've learned about world history, and what you teach me about your personal history. Make me remember you."

She paused, then smiled.

"Ready to get started?"

It wasn't a big shock that the class didn't yell "TOTALLY!" all at once, but a bunch of kids said yes, including Shelley and me. We might have said it a little louder than everyone else. Ms. Lee nodded, and as she turned and walked to the chalkboard I unfolded her note, keeping it cupped in the palm of my hand.

Hi, Chloe, would you meet me after class for a few minutes? Thanks.

FOUR

Ms. Lee wasn't lying—she spent the first day of class talking about how to do research, which was way more interesting than it sounds—and she ended class by giving us our first assignment: Ask an older family member, preferably someone from our parents' generation, to tell us an old family story, then write it down.

Simple, right? For some people, anyway.

"Think of it as your first attempt at using a primary source," she said as the bell rang. Most of the class sprinted for the door as if the room were on fire—next period was lunch—but I stayed at my desk and packed up my things more slowly.

"Can you save me a seat?" I asked Shelley as she stuffed her books into her backpack.

"You're not coming? You have to show me the, you know . . ." Shelley hitched her backpack up on one shoulder and made a scribbling motion on the palm of her hand.

"I will, but I have to talk to the teacher for a minute."

"Oh really?" Shelley did a silent smooching thing with her mouth. I grinned back and pretended to punch her on the arm as I stood up. She dodged out of the way and headed for the door, leaving me alone in the room with Ms. Lee. She was writing something in a notebook, but looked up and smiled just a little as I approached her desk. I'd been all *whatever, no problem* with Shelley, but I actually was a little bit nervous.

"Hi," I said.

"Hi, Chloe, thanks for—oh no, you look so worried!" Ms. Lee started laughing, but not in a mean way. She leaned back in her chair and looked me in the eye, laughing with her mouth open and her shoulders shaking. I also started laughing—it was impossible not to.

"So I'm NOT in trouble?" I said. Ms. Lee shook her head, her shoulders still going up and down with silent laughter.

"No, no, I'm so sorry, how could you possibly be in trouble on the first day of class?" She sat up straight again and folded her hands on the desk in front of her, but she still had a twinkly sort of look in her eye, and she stopped smiling, but it looked like she was really *trying* to not smile. She wore a ring on each of her hands, and one of them was a silhouette of a rabbit's head with orange and black stripes.

Was that a Tiger Rabbit ring? Did Ms. Lee like my favorite K-pop band too??

"I'm sorry, I should have said so anyway. I also hate to take time away from your lunch period, but I just wanted to spend a few moments chatting more privately. You have a very good reputation at this school, you know—the teachers and administrators all have great things to say about you."

"Thanks." I wasn't dumb enough to say *Of course they do*, but I thought it.

"I had a good conversation with Mr. Dombrowski."

Uh-oh.

"Oh," I said, feeling cautious. "Um . . . what did he say?"

Ms. Lee cracked a tiny smile, curling her mouth up on one side.

"He said that you were quite upset about your grade on an essay written for his class."

Upset was one way to describe it. Mr. Dombrowski was my sixth-grade English teacher, and the only teacher who's ever given me less than an A on *anything*. He gave me a B- on my personal narrative essay, which totally deserved an A, maybe an A+, and I never forgave him. I had fantasies about watching him get stampeded by a rhino, or having a tow truck dropped on his head.

"It's the only B minus I've ever gotten," I said, trying not to show any rage.

"So he told me!" Ms. Lee said, raising her eyebrows and smiling a little more broadly. "I didn't want to talk to you about that grade, however—I'm more interested in the paper itself. What was the title again?"

"*A Day in the Life of a Pseudo-Korean*," I said. "Did Mr. Dombrowski tell you why he gave me such a low grade?"

I didn't know why that made Ms. Lee smile—if she didn't think a B- was a low grade, she had to be a lousy teacher.

"He did, and—"

"How does anybody think I was being insensitive to Koreans?" I blurted out, the frustration coming back all at once. "What does he think *I* am, a Martian?"

Ms. Lee held up her hand, palm facing me, but she also nodded.

"I get it, Chloe. Mr. Dombrowski's a qualified teacher, so I know he was grading you as fairly as possible, but I understand why it bothered you."

"You do?"

Ms. Lee nodded. "I'm Korean too, you know."

I cracked a smile. "Hey, I guessed right."

"Yes. Well, I know we've just started to get to know each other, but I was born and raised in the US, so I'm no stranger to feelings of disconnection from my heritage. It's one of the reasons I studied history. I guess what I'm saying is that I'd like to encourage you to keep exploring topics like the one you wrote about, and if you ever want to discuss them with someone other than your parents—"

Ha! She obviously didn't know my parents.

"—I'm happy to meet you here during lunch, or even after school."

The tidal wave of relief that hit me was a total surprise, and I had to sit there and blink a few times before I could say anything.

"Chloe?" Ms. Lee leaned forward a little, her forehead crinkled. "Are you okay?"

"Yeah, I'm fine, that—yes. That would be great."

"Oh, good!" Ms. Lee leaned back and clapped her hands together once, like a cheerleader. "I'm excited to see what kind of work you produce this year, Chloe."

"Me too."

I really meant it! I've always liked school, but as I grabbed my backpack and headed for the door I felt more excited about Ms. Lee's class than about any class I'd ever taken.

Shelley pounced and grabbed my arm the second I got out of the classroom.

"Aaagh! Geez, what are you doing?"

"Waiting for you! What was that all about?" Shelley's eyes sparkled with curiosity.

I filled her in on all the details as we half-walked, half-ran to the lunchroom. Luckily our usual seats were still free.

"Wow, Ms. Lee seems really cool," Shelley said. The normal hurricane of cafeteria noise surrounded us as we sat down and hurried to unpack our lunches. "Are you sure it was a Tiger Rabbit ring?"

"I'm totally sure—it had the stripes and everything." I took a bite of my sandwich and pointed my chin at a table on the other side of the cafeteria, where Olivia Trilby (a seventh grader) was looking at Kyle Masterson (an eighth grader) with a facial expression that could have used a sign saying SORRY, THIS BRAIN IS TEMPORARILY OUT OF SERVICE. "You think she's been doing that the whole time?"

"Probably. She must really like you, huh?" Shelley looked down at her bag of pretzels.

"Olivia? I don't think so."

"Not Olivia, Ms. Lee."

"I guess. My turn to be teacher's pet, huh?"

I meant it as a joke, but Shelley didn't smile. Shelley

and I are best friends partly because we're the smart-est kids in school. Teachers *love* Shelley — she does all her work like I do, but she's not a loudmouth like I am, ha-ha, and she's never been in a fight. I've only been in one, but I guess that's more important than the straight As I've gotten for, oh, my entire life. Except for one totally unacceptable B-.

"Are you *mad*?" I stuck my face between Shelley's face and the table, and grinned at her from two inches away until she smiled. "Are you actually angry because a teacher likes me instead of you?"

"No, and gross, get away, your breath smells." Shelley leaned away over to the side.

"It's totally fine that you're trying to get back the teacher's pet championship, you know." I took a bite out of my apple and watched as a short-but-brutal spit-ball fight broke out three tables away. Shelley snorted.

We were still eating when the bell rang. We hadn't gone to our lockers after I talked to Ms. Lee, so we half-walked and half-ran to do that before going to next period, which was orchestra.

"Did you hear what Adam said about you?" Shelley said as we walked into the music wing, carrying our instrument cases.

"That I'm gonna destroy him in first-chair compe-tition again?"

Adam Wheeler had a fancypants expensive violin, and the fact that he could play it really, really well made it even more annoying that I had a boring, three-year-old, not-very-expensive violin, but that only made it better that I'd beaten him out for first chair every single year. He was my only real competition too. Sarah Judd liked a lot of the same books as me, but her intonation wasn't great. Charlotte Beauchamp was a great soccer player, but she was a lot better with her feet than with her hands. Jeremy Ecton was cute in a mopey kind of way, but he always cracked during competitions.

"I probably shouldn't tell you," Shelley said, looking at the ceiling. "It's kind of scary when you go into one of your rages; you look like you're about to sprout claws and fur."

"Oh ha-ha, you're sooooo funny. Come on, now you HAVE to tell me."

"I don't think he was *trying* to be a jerk, just so you know."

"Spill it!"

There was the usual bottleneck in the doorway to the orchestra room as everyone stowed their bags and stuff in the cubbies just inside the door. A second mosh pit had formed in front of the storage closets where the big instruments (cellos and basses) were kept.

A lot of the other band geeks were in hearing range, so Shelley leaned over and whispered right into my ear.

"He told Jeremy that you always win first chair because Asians all have a violin-playing gene, and how's he supposed to beat that?"

I could almost feel the surface of my eyeballs giving off steam as Shelley's words sank into my brain.

"*What?* Seriously?"

The mosh pits were breaking up as everyone headed for their seats, and after a few seconds of weaving my head to see around people I saw Adam, carrying his violin case and sitting down. In the first-chair seat. In MY seat.

"Oh, that weasel-faced little preppypants," I said, not bothering to whisper. "I don't care how expensive his violin is, he's going DOWN."

FIVE

I DIDN'T ACTUALLY WANT TO PLAY VIOLIN AT first—I was way more interested in stand-up bass. There's a Tiger Rabbit video where the whole band pretends to play stand-up bass at the same time, with a little spin-the-bass-around dance move that's just awesome. During the summer between third and fourth grades Mom took me on my first visit to String Theory, the music store and one of my favorite places in town, and when we got there I left a vapor trail as I went for the stand-up bass in the corner.

"Chloe, let's look over—"

"It's an acoustic bass, Mom! Look how big it is!" I stared up at the bass, which was probably two feet taller than I was at the time.

Mr. Smithfield, the owner of the store, had (and still has) an incredibly shiny bald head, like a skin-colored mirror. He smiled at Mom, who was in the middle of the room with her whole body tilted toward the section with the violins, and came over to me.

"Hello!" Mr. Smithfield said. He put a hand gently on the bass, like it was a person.

"Hi, how much is this bass?" I said.

"Chloe, I think you should start with something more your size—"

"You have good taste in instruments," Mr. Smithfield said. Yay for Mr. Smithfield!

"This Ferrante upright bass is a thing of beauty, isn't it?"

"Yeah."

"Your mother's right, though, it's too big for you, and it's not a starter instrument." Boo for Mr. Smithfield. He turned to Mom and did a little bow.

"What are we really thinking about for our future concert musician?"

"Violins," Mom said firmly.

"But Mom—"

"You must be big fans of Abigail Yang, HA-HA-HA!" Mr. Smithfield threw his head back when he laughed.

Mom played Abigail Yang's concert recordings all the time at home, in fact. Also Jonah Park's cello music and Jenny Chung's piano music, but twenty-two-year-old, seven-year professional Abigail Yang was the all-time classical music winner and champion at the House of Cho.

Mom nodded with a smile. "She *is* the best

violinist in the world, after all. And of course she's Korean."

"Just like me," I said, not knowing what kind of grief Abigail Yang's Korean-ness would hold for me in the future.

"Power to the Asian sisters!" Mom did a little fist pump at shoulder height, then held her hand out to me for a high five. I slapped her palm without even thinking about it.

"Mom, why can't——"

"Let's look at the violins for now, honey," Mom said in her supernicest voice, which still worked on me in the summer between third and fourth grades.

"Oh, okay," I said. The violins *were* nice, and eventually I stopped caring about the stand-up bass and started to love my violin——practicing for one to two hours per day (three before concerts) creates a bond between a musician and her instrument, you know, and back then I still thought Mom's "power to the Asian sisters" thing was funny. Then in fifth grade Adam showed up with a violin that he could barely handle and oh, the jealousy was like being stabbed in the neck with a fork.

I nodded and smiled and said "hey" to people as I homed in on Adam and his precious violin, which was probably handcrafted under a mountain by dwarves, it was so expensive. I circled around and stood in front of him, behind the big black music stand with the stenciled "GMK8" spray-painted on it, and gave him my best freeze-ray stare.

"Hey, Chloe." Adam smiled up at me, as if he wasn't a total jerk. He's shorter than me, and his eyes are weirdly far apart, but he does have a friendly smile. Jerk.

"Hey, Adam." I nudged my chin in the direction of his chair. "You're in my seat."

"Oh, I had a great summer, thanks for asking! How about you?"

"It was fine." I stabbed the air to one side with my thumb. "Out."

"Wow, who died and made you Evil Orchestra Queen?"

"Nobody. I hear you've been saying crappy stuff about me."

Adam finally stopped smiling, which made me feel better. It was harder to be mad at him when he was being all friendly like that.

"Who said that?" Adam said with a frown. "Whoever said it's a liar, I haven't ever said anything bad about you."

"It doesn't matter, just get out of my seat."

Adam leaned way back and raised both hands to face level, palms toward me.

"Whatever, Chloe. I don't know what your problem is, but here, take it."

Adam shook his head as he got up, dwarf-crafted violin in one hand and unicorn-skin violin case in the other, and moved. All the other seats were taken so he ended up sitting right next to me anyway. I heard him muttering as I got all my stuff out, and I remembered what Shelley said right before she told me what Adam said: *I don't think he was* trying *to be a jerk.*

It doesn't matter, I thought. *I don't care that he's always been friendly to me . . .*

I darted my eyes around the room without moving my head, wondering how many people were secretly thinking, *Oh look, Chloe "Tiger Girl" Cho strikes again!*

Ugh, I actually did care. I sat down, feeling like I'd just eaten something and my stomach was in the process of sending it back up.

Everyone except me and Adam was jabbering away, but things quieted down pretty fast when Mr. Coppinger, the orchestra director, came out of his office and stood in front of the room. Mr. C was one of the rare teachers who most of the kids in school actually liked enough to listen to.

"Welcome back, troops!" Mr. C said in his booming voice. He's pretty short and skinny, so it's always kind of a surprise to be reminded how loud his voice is. "Nice to see so many familiar faces, even those of you bold enough to claim first chairs before we've had any actual competitions."

He looked at me and waggled his fuzzy brown eyebrows. I smirked, and he smirked back. That smirk was the kind of thing that made kids like him.

"Let's cut right to the chase." Mr. C brought his hands together with a loud SMACK, then rubbed them together like he was trying to start a fire. He grinned, reached into his back pocket, and pulled out his conductor's baton.

"Oh, I just know everyone's been practicing this summer. Chloe, you've been doing your best Abigail Yang impression, right?"

Sigh. I looked over my shoulder at Shelley, who was two rows back with the other viola players. She very slowly put one palm over her face. Mr. C is cool, but every year it's the same Abigail Yang thing. At least he was consistent.

"Oh, I don't have to do an impression—I just act like myself, since we're practically twins."

I tried not to let *all* the sarcasm show in my voice, but I don't think I made it. I heard Shelley give a muffled snort.

"Okay then, before we get started let's take care of some business. First let's welcome all of our new musicians. This is officially the biggest the George Matthew K through 8 Orchestra has ever been!"

Everyone started clapping, and I (and all the other returning orchestra members) looked around. There were at least ten new faces, including a couple of people's little brothers and sisters I recognized from around town. They were probably all fifth graders, but they looked like they were in kindergarten. Little kids. I sniffed.

"I know all you old-timers will help our newbies learn the ropes. Make them feel welcome, okay?"

"Oh, definitely," Todd Schumacher said with an evil hoot.

"Be nice," Mr. C said. "Moving on! Like every year, we'll have first-chair competitions starting in a couple of weeks."

The room broke out in applause again. This time I turned all the way around to look at Shelley. She pointed at me two times, really hard, like she was trying to stab me with her finger. I pointed at myself and made a wide-eyed who-me? face.

Mr. C held up both index fingers and raised his eyebrows.

"So here's how it's going to work."

Mr. C gave a rundown of the first-chair challenge process. First chair for every section is up for grabs at the start of every year. If you want it, you sign up to compete for it. Everybody who signs up plays the same piece for Mr. C. The person who gives the best performance, aka me in the violin section, wins first chair, which means playing the first-chair parts on all the songs (harder, but more interesting), and playing all the solos (totally fun and exciting).

"And I know some of you grizzled orchestra veterans think it'll be a piece of cake to win first chair like you did last year, but don't get cocky. I just know everyone practiced really, really hard over the summer, correct?"

Mr. C fake-frowned in a way that made all of the hair on his head look like a single huge clump. Everyone laughed. Mr. C glanced quickly at me, then to my right. I glanced that way too—Adam looked excited, and when I caught his eye he gave me a stare I recognized. It was his I'm-totally-going-to-win stare. I smirked back as Mr. C rubbed his hands together.

"Now that we've got that out of the way, let's get started! Take out the first piece in your folders and . . ."

As the sound of rustling sheet music filled the room, Adam leaned just barely in my direction—a millimeter or two, no more—and whispered, "You're going down this year, Cho."

I snort-laughed. "In your dreams, Wheeler."

"Sure, whatever. I'm just saying." Adam started tuning his violin with a smile.

I started tuning up too, not even a little bit worried. The only thing that would keep me from winning first chair would be getting abducted by aliens. It was a done deal.

SIX

WALKING TO DAD'S FISH STORE TAKES FIFTEEN minutes longer than it does to walk straight home, but asking for a new violin is always a high-priority thing, so I made the hike to downtown Primrose Heights.

Aquariums Unlimited doesn't look like much from the outside — there's a pile of dusty-looking fish tanks in the single tall window, and the sign with the picture of a fancy goldfish hanging over the door is faded — but once you get inside it's pretty great. The store is kind of like a big hallway. It's not very wide, but it goes way back into the building. It's really hot in there, so everyone who works there wears T-shirts and shorts most of the time. Dad wears pants because he's the boss, I guess.

I pushed the door open and walked in, passing the cash register on the left and the rows of saltwater tanks on the right.

"Chloe! What's up, dream girl?" Darren Speck started working for Dad in high school and never stopped — he'd been there for five years in all. He smiled, winked, AND pointed at me with his hands shaped like finger guns, because he's just that cheesy.

"Ew, I'm not your dream girl," I said, smiling back at him. "Is my dad here?"

"He's in back with a customer, but I think — yup, here he comes. Hi, Mr. Dietz, can I ring that up for you?"

Mr. Dietz (father of backup soccer goalie Jill Dietz) plopped a couple of water-filled plastic bags on the counter. He glanced at me, raised an eyebrow as if I was doing something strange by just being there, and turned back to Darren. It wasn't like Mr. Dietz and I had pinky promised to be best friends forever, but if I was a cat I would have puffed up my tail and bared my claws.

When I was little and school was closed for some reason — teacher training, yeti sightings, or whatever — I would sometimes spend a big chunk of the day at the store with Dad, partly because it meant no babysitters, and partly because I just loved it there. On one of those days in second grade Mr. Dietz came into the store with a giant sack of plants. I was reading a book in the office with the door open, so I had a direct line of sight to Dad behind the counter and a partial view of Mr. Dietz in front of it.

"I don't appreciate having to come back like this, you know."

Nice. Not even a lousy "hello" from Mr. Dietz.

"Stan, like I said on Sunday, you were here as a vendor. Customers who are spending money in the store have priority over vendors. You can understand that."

Mr. Dietz grumbled something under his breath.

"Stan." Dad planted his hands on the counter. "Come on. Lick the fish or lick the bait, it's—"

"Lick the fish or lick the bait?"

I wouldn't have admitted it for a million dollars, but I felt as confused as Mr. Dietz sounded when he said that. Lick the fish? What the heck was Dad talking about?

"Uh, I mean—"

"Fish or cut bait? Is that what you're trying to say?" Okay, Mr. Dietz sounded way nastier than he needed to. It wasn't like Dad had punched him in the face.

"Yes, that's what I mean. Fish or cut bait."

"What is that, some kind of *translation* problem?"

Why was Mr. Dietz being such a crabbyface?

"You could say that." Dad was . . . smiling. Like he was laughing at a private joke.

"Well, all I can say is they have some strange sayings in China—"

I was super confused. Why was he talking about China? I must have made some kind of noise, because Mr. Dietz paused and Dad looked at me.

"Dad, why is he talking about Chi—"

"Chloe." Dad held up one index finger in a just-a-second gesture. "I'm talking with Mr. Dietz."

"But—"

"Later, honey. I'm sorry, Stan, let's see what you've got."

Mr. Dietz muttered under his breath again as he set his plants on the counter, and I closed the office door so I wouldn't have to hear him talk about his plants, which were probably all about to die anyway. When Mr. Dietz left, another customer came in and asked Dad about setting up a saltwater reef aquarium, and in the end we never did talk about the Chinese thing.

Since then I'd managed to never be in the store at the same time as Mr. Dietz, a streak I would have been happy to keep going, so I looked away from him with a toss of my head and went up the short staircase that led to the back of the store. Most of the actual fish were back there, starting with a huge, waist-high tank full of plants right in front of the stairs. As I climbed the steps Dad came into view over the top of that tank, standing on a stepladder and draining water out of a tank on a higher shelf. He smiled as I walked around the big plant tank. The aquarium he was working on had a bunch of tiny loaches in it, and he was careful not to catch any of them in the end of the vacuum/ siphon gizmo he was using to drain the tank.

"Hi, sweetie, are you here to help me with inventory?"

"Dad. No. You're the boss, you're supposed to keep track of my work schedule." I shifted my violin from one hand to the other.

"Yes, but how could I keep track of it in a way that's more reliable than asking you?" Dad smiled as he coiled up the siphon gizmo's long plastic tube, stepped down from the ladder, and picked up the bucket of fish-poop water. "You and that positronic brain of yours."

As usual, I was both embarrassed and happy about Dad cracking one of his lame science-fiction jokes.

"Well then, since you're here, can you at least feed the frogs?" Dad said as he carried the bucket to the big sink at the back of the store and poured the poop water into it.

"Well, that depends, Dad, are you gonna pay me?"

"Have I ever not paid you?"

I snorted, because I was never, ever going to let

him forget the one time he tried to pay me with ice cream instead of money.

"How about if you just buy me a new violin?" I said as I grabbed an apron from the hooks next to the sink. I went into the back room, which is crammed full of all kinds of stuff, including the refrigerator and freezer. I grabbed a blister pack of frozen bloodworms out of the freezer.

"—one you have?" Dad said.

"Sorry, what?"

"I said, what's wrong with the one you have?"

I popped one of the little red balls of worm directly into the tank. The frogs swam up, kicking their legs and looking like they were flying instead of swimming, and chomped crazily on the frozen ball, which started shedding pieces of worm in all directions.

"It's old."

"I thought violins get better with age."

"Dad, I've had this one for *three years*!"

"Oh NO," Dad said, holding his hands up next to his face and shaking them as he made a goofy, wide-eyed face.

"Cut it out! I deserve a new violin, don't you think? I've been first chair for three years in a row!"

"Wait, did you get first chair again already?" Dad

dried his hands off with a gross-looking towel. "They do that on the first day of school now?"

"No, it's later, but I'll win." It's not bragging if it's true, you know.

"No one can ever criticize you for lack of confidence," Dad said with a smile. "We really don't have room in the budget for a new violin, sweetie."

"They're not that expensive," I said, which wasn't a total lie — new violins are super expensive, but I'd been looking into other options. "Not if I get a used one."

"We've been down that road before, honey; you weren't happy with any of the used ones except for Adam Wheeler's, and you refused to get that one, remember?"

"That was *here*, Dad, in Primrose Heights. Why don't we go to the city and get one?"

Did I mention that I've never been to Capital City even though it's only an hour away from our house? *Never?*

Dad blew out a big *whoosh* of breath, puffing out his cheeks in the process.

"Please? Daddy?"

"Oh, it's 'DADDY' now, is it?" Dad chuckled. "I'll think about it, okay?"

"Yay! Do you know if there are any Korean restaurants there?"

"Oh, well, I don't know, honey." Dad turned away and started filling the bucket with clean water. He tipped a capful of something from a plastic bottle into the bucket as it filled. "I haven't been to Capital City in months, you know."

Oh, it was *that* tone of voice, the I-don't-actually-want-to-talk-about-this tone of voice. My shoulders clenched.

"Does Mom know any Korean restaurants in Capital City?"

"You'll have to ask your mother about that," Dad said as he started siphoning the bucket of clean water back into the loach tank. The loaches went off in all directions, wiggling along in their snake-like way.

"Dad, why don't you ever talk about Korea?"

Sometimes you just have to get things right out there in the open, you know what I mean?

"What do you mean?" Dad hopped down from the ladder and disappeared into the back room with the bucket and siphon. Geez, the only thing worse than a clueless dad is a dad who pretends to not know what his own daughter is talking about and then RUNS

AWAY. I didn't feel like letting him escape, so I followed him in there, then had to back up when he came right back out.

"I mean, why don't you ever talk about Korea? I ask you stuff and you totally ignore me!"

Dad stopped, still facing away from me, and put his hands on his hips. He blew out a long breath, turned around, pulled the stepladder away from the loach tank, and sat on it.

"Aren't parents supposed to be happy when their kids want to talk about stuff like this? Why aren't you happy??" I crossed my arms. The apron made a plasticky crinkle sound against my chest.

"Chloe, I'm happy, honestly. And I'm not trying to ignore you, it's just . . ."

"It's just that you ARE."

"It's not that simple, honey. Talking about Korea . . . it's complicated, and painful."

"So what? I'm not in kindergarten, you know."

"Yes, I know."

"Our new social studies teacher said she *admires* my interest in being Korean."

"Oh really?" Dad sat up a little straighter. "Why does she feel that way?"

"Because she's Korean, Dad. Duh."

That REALLY got Dad's attention. He actually stood up and started pacing. There wasn't that much room between the rows of aquariums, though, so he looked a little bit like a character from an old video game, zinging back and forth really fast.

"It's in the letter we got from the school, Dad. Why are you doing that?"

"Doing what?" Dad looked down at his feet and stopped. "Oh. I'm just . . . surprised. She's really from Korea?"

"Well, no, she said she was born in America."

Dad put a hand over his mouth and stared at me with his eyes narrowed.

"Dad? You're kind of freaking me out."

Dad snapped his hand shut and shook his head quickly, like he was trying to shake off something that had landed on it. "I'm sorry, honey. That's great that your teacher is encouraging you."

"You sure?" I said, my arms still crossed.

"Really."

"Great, because I need your help with our first assignment!"

"You need—"

Dad was sadly mistaken if he thought I was giving him a chance to say no that soon.

"I made a copy of the assignment for you," I said, shoving a crisply folded sheet of paper into his hand. "It's easy, we just have to get a family member to tell us a family story, preferably from a noncontemporary time period."

"Oh." Dad took the paper, mostly because I'd actually gotten it to go between his thumb and index finger. "Wait, your teacher gave you an assignment that requires your parents to participate? That doesn't sound right to me —"

"I talked to her about it after class." Which was technically true, if you defined "it" as *the family narrative* instead of *an assignment that requires your parents to participate.* "And it can be any family member, not just parents, but . . ."

Dad sighed.

"Chloe, I don't think —"

"Hey, Mr. Cho?" Darren's upper half came into view at the top of the stairs. "There's a call for you, from that sleazeball discus breeder."

"Thanks, Darren." Dad quickly metronomed his head between me and Darren a couple of times.

"I gotta go, Dad, homework and stuff! Bye!" I weaved around his outstretched hands, which he'd stuck out about halfway in my direction, stood on tiptoes, kissed his cheek, and bolted down the stairs.

"Bye, Darren!" I yelled as I ran past the counter. I went fast enough that his "See you, Chloe" was cut off by the door closing behind me.

Don't give them a chance to say no, I thought. *Don't give them a chance to say no.*

Next up: Mom.

SEVEN

WHEN I WAS NINE I TRIED TO CONVINCE MOM TO buy me a pet iguana. I pulled out all the stops— crying, bargaining, cleaning my room without being told, everything. No luck. I could tell Dad was kind of into the idea, which was why we ended up getting Kaa instead. I learned a few things. Iguanas grow to be six feet long, which is huge; ball pythons grow to be four feet long, but spend most of their time curled up in balls (*ball* python, get it?); and if you harass your parents long enough to get you something they really don't want to get you, they might end up getting you something else that's almost as good.

Trading down from a new violin to help with my family narrative assignment; that would have been my strategy, and the best part was that it was only tempo-rarily giving up my quest for a new violin. No way would Mom and Dad ever get mad at me about that. The worst they could do was keep saying no. Of course,

I didn't know Dad had already called Mom and messed it all up before I could even try.

"Hi, Mom, can—" I said when she got home from work, but she was way ahead of me.

"Hi, sweetie." Mom was in her no-important-meetings work clothes—black T-shirt, matching gray cardigan and skirt, and black boots. She was stylish in a mom kind of way, I guess. "Sorry to interrupt you, but I have some great news!"

"Okay, but first I want to—"

Mom kept talking as she walked into the living room and put her laptop bag on the coffee table.

"I just talked to your dad—we know you've been playing a starter violin this whole time, but we just haven't been able to afford the kind of quality instrument you really want. Well, today I found out that I'm getting a bonus at work!"

!!!

"Wait, does that mean . . ."

Mom smiled, nodded, and put her hands on my cheeks, which I usually pretend not to like even though I do like it, but which I couldn't even pretend to not like at that moment.

"Want to go buy a new violin?"

"You mean right now?"

Mom let go of my cheeks, raised her hand up to eye level, and jingled her car keys.

"I'm not holding these for show."

Wow. Two years of asking for a new violin, TWO YEARS, and just like that I was getting a new one! I totally forgot about primary source family stories and new teachers who were Korean as Mom and I got into the car and drove to the other side of town to String Theory.

There was already a bunch of kids and their parents in the store when we got there, mostly littler kids, although there was a high school guy whose name I couldn't remember looking at ukuleles.

"Over here!" I dragged Mom past the guitar, drum, and woodwind sections to the back, where the orchestra stuff was. String Theory has a whole room just for violins, violas, cellos, my old friend the stand-up bass, and even a giant harp. Mr. Smithfield was already in the room, doing something to a cello with his back to us. He turned and smiled, partly at my mom but mostly at me.

Wait for it, I thought.

"Why, it's our own little Abigail Yang!"

Oh, for crying out loud.

"Yeah, I'm like her in garden gnome form," I said. "I'm so tiny."

"We're here to get Chloe a new violin," Mom said, putting her arm around me and squeezing my shoulder in a cut-it-out way. Mom doesn't really wear perfume, but she smelled good anyway, kind of leafy-smelling.

"Wonderful news!" Mr. Smithfield raised his long, bony arms in front of himself and clasped his fists together in a show of dorky enthusiasm. "What are we thinking about?"

"Chloe?" Mom said, looking at me with a smile. I stared at her for a second, not getting it, then suddenly I got it.

"What, you're gonna let me pick?"

"Well, I have to approve your choice, of course. We're not buying a Stradivarius or a del Gesù."

"An easy decision, since I don't have any in the store!" Mr. Smithfield barked like a seal at his own joke. I resisted the urge to slap myself on the forehead.

"They say those old Italian violins don't sound any better than new ones anyway," I said.

"Well, I don't know about that, but we have some terrific new instruments here," Mr. Smithfield said. He rubbed his stubbly chin, patted his round belly, and reached for one of the violins hanging on the wall. "I think this one right here might be a good choice for you—give it a try!"

Mr. Smithfield handed me the violin, and after I took it with both hands he opened a drawer and took out a bow. "I put fresh rosin on this just today."

Oh, I should have brought my own bow. Stupid. I shifted the violin into my left hand and took the bow in my right hand, carefully arranging my fingers in the right places. With the violin securely parked on my shoulder and tucked under my chin, I played a couple of open strings just to find out what the overall sound was like. I knew right away that I didn't want this one. The A string didn't exactly howl, but there was definitely a wobbly, in-and-out sound to it, like it was fading out right on the beat.

"Ugh, this has a wolf tone," I said.

"Chloe," Mom said in her watch-*your*-tone voice.

"Well, it does!"

"Oh, that's too bad," Mr. Smithfield said. "That's a Shan Jiang, they're very good instruments for the price. Chinese, you know."

He looked at us with a big smile, like he was giving us a birthday present or something. I was tempted to whack him over the head with the crappy violin, but then I'd have to buy it.

"We're Kore—" I started, but Mom cut me off.

"That's very thoughtful, Mr. Smithfield—"

THOUGHTFUL? Was Mom out of her mind?

"—but it's not necessary; we can loosen the purse strings a little."

"We can?" I said. What was going on with Mom? Did someone hit her on the head with a magic money-spending stick?

"Oh, that's tremendous, just tremendous!" Mr. Smithfield said. "I always try to work with families on a budget, of course, but you know, there's nothing quite like the experience of playing a really good, high-end instrument. Let's see, let's see . . ."

I pointed at a violin in the top row.

"I want to try that one."

Mr. Smithfield looked at me with his eyebrows raised all the way up to the top of his head, then crossed his arms.

"Really now," he said, still smiling. "Because that is exactly the violin I was going to suggest next."

He used a stepladder to get the violin down. It was lighter than the other violins, more yellowish than red, with a glossy finish. I looked up at Mom and leaned against her, bouncing up and down a little in excitement, and she smiled down at me, although there was a little something in her facial expression that I couldn't figure out.

I stepped out from under Mom's arm as Mr. Smithfield held the violin out in both hands, like he was handing me a magic sword or something. I took it and turned it over so I could see the grain of the wood on the back.

"Beauty, isn't it?" Mr. Smithfield said. "That's a DeSio, they make excellent violins. Unusual to find an instrument with a spruce back, but it sounds terrific. I wish more luthiers would apply a clear coat like this one did."

I got the violin into position, raised the bow, took a breath, then played a nice slow G scale. The notes spilled out of the violin strings like beams of sunlight, and I got that tingly feeling I always get when I'm playing something as well as I can play, except I was just playing a scale!

I paused for a second. Mom reached past my shoulder, quickly picked up the price tag hanging from the scroll of the DeSio, and just as quickly dropped it. I looked back at her, but she was still smiling. A good sign.

"Do you know—" Mr. Smithfield said, but I was already launching into the etude we'd warmed up with all through sixth grade. I hadn't played it in months, but I'd had it note-perfect at the end of the school year, and it wasn't a very hard piece, so it came right back.

"Bravo!" Mr. Smithfield said as he and Mom clapped loudly. "That was marvelous! Nothing like a good etude!"

I smiled happily, then slid my eyes over to Mom. I gave her my sad-puppy-dog face, just to cover all the bases, and she burst out laughing. Mom has the best laugh—loud, but not too loud, and she gets her whole upper body into it. She turned to Mr. Smithfield.

"Well, Mr. Smithfield, it looks like I'm buying a yellow violin today."

"An excellent, excellent choice." Mr. Smithfield clasped both of Mom's hands in his and pumped them up and down a bunch of times, grinning and bobbing his head. "It'll become a family heirloom, I'm sure."

"I certainly hope so," Mom said with a smile. She put her hands on her hips and gave Mr. Smithfield a fake frown. "Now, I suppose we should get down to negotiating. That price IS a little too high for comfort."

"Oh, it's a perfectly fair price, but we might be able to work something out. I have the perfect case for it, by the way, let me just get that . . ."

Mr. Smithfield and Mom walked across the store to a pile of assorted instrument cases, and I trailed along behind them, running my hands over my beautiful new violin.

Adam Wheeler was going to be SO jealous.

EIGHT

OH MY GOD, THE NEW VIOLIN WAS AMAZING. I could have hung up posters on the walls of the orchestra practice rooms, I spent so much time in them. I probably didn't need to put rosin on the bow and strings every time, but why leave stuff like that to chance, am I right? I'd lobbied for the yellow fiberglass case, but not too hard, since I knew that even after bargaining with Mr. Smithfield the violin itself still cost a LOT. It was actually a little hard to leave it in my locker. I even practiced before breakfast a couple of times.

I told Shelley the story as we walked to school the next day.

". . . so I had to get the less expensive case, but I got the violin and it's just as good as we thought it'd be!"

"That is so AWESOME," Shelley said as the school came into view a couple of blocks in the distance. "But why did she suddenly change her mind?"

"She said she got a bonus at work."

"Does she spend all her work bonuses on you?"

I shrugged. "She's never mentioned getting a bonus before."

I didn't forget about Ms. Lee's assignment—that'd be like forgetting to breathe oxygen—and if I ever needed proof that Mom and Dad had some kind of private, two-person conspiracy against me, trying to do that assignment was it. I asked at breakfast a couple of days later.

"Dad, I need to do that family story assignment—"

"I'm sorry, honey, I'm running really late this morning!" BAM, Dad flew out the door like a super-hero. A superhero who's avoiding his own daughter.

I asked Mom that day after school.

"Mom, did Dad tell you about the family sto—"

"Oh, Chloe, I completely forgot, let me show you what I picked up on my way home!"

Mom, who I later realized hadn't forgotten anything since I'd just gotten home from school, half-walked and half-ran into her bedroom before I could even finish what I was saying.

"—ry. MOM! I'm asking you a que—"

"Ta-da!" Mom came back into the living room holding a new violin bow in her outstretched hands. A new bow!

"Is that a Fresco bow??" I said, clapping my hands together in spite of myself. "A carbon-fiber Fresco?"

"It sure is." Mom actually kneeled down and held the bow out to me like it was a sword or something, and I gently picked it up. The Fresco water-droplet logo on the heel was inlaid with abalone—so pretty—and I rubbed it with my thumb as I tested the balance of the bow. It was just the right weight, and it was going to look fantastic paired with the new violin.

So, that happened, which meant I spent the rest of the night practicing (and maybe looking at myself holding the new violin and the new bow in the mirror once or twice), and I totally forgot to ask about the assignment that night. Or the next night.

Mom is an evil genius.

In fact, I didn't remember until the day before the assignment was due, mostly because of important matters of fashion. This was the first time I could remember being even more excited about the second week of school than the first, and it wasn't just because of my new violin and bow. I decided to wear my hanbok, the one I'd saved up for almost a year to buy. I'd been reserving it for my birthday, when I planned to make my next try at convincing Mom and Dad to take Shelley and me to the city for Korean food, but hey, sometimes a girl needs to change the plan.

Dad didn't say anything except "Chloe, breakfast," when he first came into my room, but when he saw me obsessively checking myself out in the mirror he stopped and smiled.

"You look beautiful, honey," he said. "That is one fancy dress."

"Thanks," I said, frowning at myself in the mirror as I twisted and turned. I ran a finger under the dark purple collar of the jeogori (basically a lavender-colored jacket that ended right below my chest), plucked at my shoulders to make the jeogori sleeves a little puffier, and ran my hands over the dark purple fabric of the skirt, which had a semi-complicated pattern of round flowers and swirly lines.

It was the most fantastic outfit I'd ever worn. I looked *good*.

"Breakfast," Dad said. He turned my shoulders until my top half was facing the door. I walked out with him, pivoting my top half back toward the mirror for one last look.

Okay, super-whatever reaction from Dad; how was Mom going to react? Would it be as big of a disaster as the last time we'd gone shopping, which was a year ago?

"How about this?" Mom had said, pulling a tie-dyed shirt off of a rack. (Seriously, how did tie-dyed shirts become THE THING TO WEAR at school?)

"No, Mom. Just because the entire school's going to look like a lava lamp doesn't mean I have to."

"Oh come on, you've always been ahead of the curve with clothes, right?"

It was a mystery how anyone could say that about me when there were people in school like Jenny Barton, who really was ahead of the curve with her superclunky boots and wild color schemes. I was just a fashion lemming, and I hadn't really gotten it until then.

"Where do you buy your clothes, Mom?" I said, taking a big step away from the tie-dyed shirts. "Can I get my clothes there?"

"It's just a boring store for grown-ups," Mom said.

"It can't be any more boring than this place . . ."

It was true that Mom's clothes were kind of boring, but at least they were different from what everyone else at school would be wearing. Then inspiration struck.

"Wait, are there any Korean stores in the city?" I said.

"Korean . . . stores . . ."

"You know, stores that sell stuff from the country you were born in? Power to the Asian sisters and all that stuff?"

"Chloe, really, let's just—"

"Hello, you two look a little bit lost!"

Mom and I both twitched in surprise. The sales-person who approached us was new, or at least some-one I hadn't seen before.

"Back to school, am I right?" she said.

"Right," Mom said. "I understand tie-dyed is what the kids are wearing this year."

"I don't care, Mom."

"Of course you don't," the clerk said, almost too cheerfully. "Why would you? I've read that *Japanese Schoolgirl Alert* blog; you girls are way ahead of the rest of us in style, technology, everything!"

"Um, we're not Japane—"

"We don't have anything as fun as the stuff in *Japanese Schoolgirl Alert*, but, hmm. There are some cute *Aoshima Island* T-shirts—"

T-shirts from a cartoon show about an island pop-ulated by funny cats would have been great if I was five years old, and I didn't feel like being all ironic and stuff, so no.

"Do you have any Tiger Rabbit shirts?" I asked.

"Ummm, I don't think so, is that a TV show?"

"No—well, yeah, but they're really a K-pop group."

"K-pop." The clerk rubbed her cheek with one hand. "K-pop . . ."

"Chloe, are you sure you don't like—"

"YES, MOTHER, I'M SURE. I DON'T LIKE THE FLOWER POWER THING."

"Hey. WATCH YOUR TONE."

At least four girls in butt-ugly shirts turned and stared. Their moms (and one random dad) turned and stared too.

"Mom, *please* can we go to—"

"We're not going anywhere unless you get yourself under control—"

"Why can't I buy clothes I actually want to wear instead of—"

And thus went the rest of the day, even after I finally picked out a bunch of all-black clothes just because I couldn't go to school naked. I'd wondered if Mom was worried the mean girls of Primrose Heights would put a target on my forehead for wearing non-boring, Korean-style clothes. Or maybe she just really, really liked tie-dyed stuff. It was point-of-no-return time, so I was about to find out.

Dad herded me into the kitchen, parked me in my chair, and kissed me on the head as usual. He sat in the chair to my left and started in on his eggs, while I carefully started spreading butter on a piece of toast. I was too worried about spilling food on my dress to go for the jam.

"Wow," Mom said in a not-actually-wow way. "You look . . . huh."

"Gee, Mom, don't overdo it with the compliments." I looked straight at my cup as I drank some milk, sticking my face out over the table in case of spills. Mom took a dainty little bite of egg as she stared at my hanbok.

"I thought you were saving that dress for your birthday party."

I felt a tiny spark of irritation as I used my knife to saw up a slice of bacon and stabbed the pieces one by one with a fork. No point in taking the risk of getting bacon grease on my hands, right?

"I want to show it to Ms. Lee. I think she might like it."

"Mmmm."

"Because she's Korean too, Mom."

"Oh, she'll like it fine," Mom said, totally dodging the Korean thing. Her phone was on the table next to her coffee. It vibrated, and she peered at it as she forked up another bite of egg. "Will you be able to play your violin while you're wearing that dress?"

"I don't know. Can you tell it's a hanbok?" I said, looking down at the table. A direct question about something Korean! Danger, Chloe Cho, danger!

"What's a hanbok?" Mom said, still looking at her phone.

I coughed, spitting out a few bacon bits, thumping my hands on the table, and almost knocking over Dad's coffee. He smoothly grabbed the cup and lifted it up and in the opposite direction from me.

"Oh great," I said, picking three chewed-up crumbs of pig flesh off of my lap.

"That's why we use napkins," Dad said, taking a slug from his rescued coffee.

"Mom. You know, a hanbok?" I said, picking at imaginary bacon stains on my dress—I couldn't see any actual stains, but still. Stupid bacon. Lucky for me I'd bought the purple hanbok instead of the white one.

Mom looked up from her phone with a totally blank expression. She had no idea what I was talking about.

"Hanbok? A Korean dress?"

"OH!" Mom said suddenly. She let out a laugh that was WAY too loud. "Oh, honey, of course I know what a hanbok is. It's just been such a long time since I've worn one!"

I leaned back in my chair and stared at her. Why did it matter how long it'd been? I was positive I wouldn't ever forget what a *dress* is.

"Did you guys wear hanboks when you got

married?" I asked. "Isn't that how they did it in, you know, the old days?"

"You make us sound like dinosaurs," Dad said through a mouthful of bacon.

"Chew with your mouth closed, Dad. Mom, come on, did you wear—"

"Honey, I can't talk about this now, I'm in a hurry—"

"It's a yes-or-no question, Mom."

"Chloe, I don't want to talk about it," Mom said. "It's too . . ."

Painful, hard, yadda yadda yadda . . .

". . . painful. Those were hard times. Let's look forward, not backward."

AGH! So frustrating!

"But—"

"I can't be late today," Mom said in a businesslike tone as she stood up and grabbed her plate. "This will probably be my only chance to talk directly with the VP of Finance all semester."

"You too, Chloe," Dad said as I tracked Mom into the kitchen with my eyes. She wouldn't look at me, of course.

"Dad, do you—"

"I can't take you today, honey, I'm sorry," he said. "You'll be late if you don't get a move on."

"All right, all right . . ."

Mom cruised back through the dining room as I was taking my plate to the sink.

"Bye, honey, have a great day," she said, clasping my shoulder and kissing my temple.

"Yeah yeah, you too."

"Hey," Dad said as Mom kissed his cheek. "Tone."

"My tone is good, I have a good tone, good-bye," I grumbled as Mom blew out the front door. Dad hurried over to kiss me on the head, then he was out the door too. My parents, masters of the disappearing act.

I locked the door behind me as I left. Halfway to the sidewalk I stopped, stood up straighter, and lifted my chin. I was wearing my new fusion hanbok, inspired by the wardrobe of Hyungsook Lee, lead vocalist of K-pop band Tiger Rabbit. Time to be awesome.

"Power to the Asian sisters," I muttered, then headed to Shelley's house, one hand clenched in a fist, the other holding the handle to my new violin case.

NINE

"OH MY GOD YOU LOOK AMAZING!" SHELLEY shrieked as she stepped out her front door. Mrs. Dubose, the Drakes' next-door neighbor, looked up from her flower bed. I raised my hand in a hey-Mrs-Dubose gesture, and she waved back.

"That's such a pretty dress, Chloe!" she said. "It's so . . . exotic!"

Heavy sigh.

"Thanks, Mrs. D," I said, not even trying to keep the sarcasm out of my voice as Shelley ran out to the sidewalk to meet me.

"YOU LOOK JUST LIKE HYUNGSOOK LEE!" Shelley said, clapping her hands and hopping in place.

"Can you say that a little louder? I think one of my eardrums is still intact."

"Sorry, sorry, but I thought you were—"

"Saving it for my birthday party, I know."

"You're totally kissing up to Ms. Lee, aren't you?" Shelley crossed her arms, puckered her mouth up on one side, and tapped her foot.

"NO."

Shelley grinned. "Suck-up."

"Oh, I'M a suck-up? Who sent Christmas cards to every teacher in school two years ago?"

Shelley shrugged. "It was worth a try."

The good thing about actually walking through the door at school with a new outfit on is that it's too late to do anything about it, and once I could stare people down I instantly felt less nervous. If I had a dollar for every time someone whispered behind their hand at the sight of my dress that morning, I could have bought another dress. And maybe some shoes.

Lindsay "Dull Knife" Crisp actually gave me a compliment that sounded real, which was nice, but the only person besides Shelley whose opinion I really cared about was Ms. Lee, so I got nervous again when we filed into social studies. I tried to catch Ms. Lee's eye as we sat down, but she was all business as she got up from her desk with a stack of handouts in her hands.

"Good morning, class!" she said. "Let's get right into it, shall we? We're going to spend the next few weeks working on a very exciting project—"

There was a wave of murmurs, grunts, and one clearly audible groan. Slackers.

" —and I know you're all entirely capable of doing a great job on it. It's going to be a lot of work, but it's also going to be a lot of fun."

Ms. Lee started putting a bunch of handouts on the front seat of every row of desks. She did look right at me when she handed me my stack, but she was still talking, so it was one of those generic I'm-looking-at-the-whole-class looks. I might as well have been wearing a garbage bag. I got a sinking feeling in the middle of my body, like someone had just dumped a brick into my stomach.

We're in the middle of class, I reminded myself. *She's TEACHING.* Then I looked at the handout, which was more like a booklet, and realized she was assigning us a really cool project.

The Model United Nations Handbook.

"Country analysis is one of the major components of this class. We're going to do intensive research on individual countries, including their governments, histories, cultures, traditions, food, lifestyles, and more. You'll need all that information to serve as those nations' foreign ambassadors. Some of you will represent a country that's part of your own ancestry, but most of you won't, just because there are only so many Western European countries to go around, but don't worry, it won't affect your grade."

Ms. Lee smiled. "Don't forget about your first assignment, of course. You all remember that's due tomorrow, right?"

I had a brief moment of panic. Doing an assignment at the last minute! Was I losing my edge?

"I've assigned each of you a country." Ms. Lee picked a stack of envelopes off of her desk and held the top one up. "These are letters officially welcoming you as your country's ambassador, and inviting you to our UN General Assembly, which is when your final, joint presentations are due."

Joint presentations, eh?

"Please come up and accept your letter when your name is called. Kevin Archer!"

As Kevin went slouching up to the front of the room I flipped open my booklet to the first page.

An Introduction to the
MODEL UNITED NATIONS

The key to being a successful Model UN delegate is thorough preparation. There are five steps that should be taken before the conference. It is our suggestion that the five main areas of study be addressed in the following order, as each area is progressively more in-depth than the one listed before:

- *Structure and history of the United Nations*
- *Your assigned member state or nongovern-mental organization*
- *Your committee*
- *Your role in the committee*
- *Agenda topics beyond what is written in the background guides*

"Chloe Cho!"

I snapped to attention. Since I was right there in the front row it was easy for Ms. Lee to hand my letter right to me, which she did in a superbusiness-like way before moving right on to the next name.

"Shelley Drake!"

I opened my envelope as Ms. Lee was handing Shelley hers. There was a single sheet of paper inside.

From the Desk of the Secretary-General:
Congratulations on your appointment as the United Nations delegate for South Korea.

!!!

There was no way it could be an accident I'd been given South Korea, right? I looked at Ms. Lee with a superdopey grin on my face, but she was still calling out names.

"Chase Edwards!"

Whatever, I was still happy. I actually wiggled in my seat with happiness.

"*Pssst!*"

I turned toward Shelley to see her waving her letter in my face.

"I got France!" she said, keeping her voice down but not whispering. "How did she know I'm a quarter French?"

I shrugged. "Lucky guess? I got South Korea."

"Well, yeah," Shelley said. "You only had a whole conversation about it."

"Emily Neilson!"

As Ms. Lee kept going through the alphabet, people started making comments about their country assignments.

"*Turkey?* Aw, man . . ."

"Is Micronesia even a real country?"

"New Zealand, awesome! Hobbit movies!"

"Tom Wolcott!"

Ms. Lee handed Tom his envelope and waited as

everyone waved their letters around and squawked like parakeets.

"OKAY!" she said after a minute, loud enough that everyone shut up right away. "There are two things I want you to know before we really dig in to the structure of this project. One, you'll be working in teams—the research you do on your country will include its diplomatic relationship with your team-mate's country."

The class's lazy population (most of the class, in other words) groaned out loud. I could practically read their minds—*Oh no, twice as much work, Ms. Lee is so mean!* Weaklings. I reached out with my left hand without looking and sure enough, Shelley's fist bumped mine right on cue.

"Two, your research should definitely include one aspect of your country that you're particularly inter-ested in, whether it's something like baseball—"

Ms. Lee nodded at Eric Snyder, who wore baseball jerseys every day except for the days when he wore football jerseys. Eric pumped his fist. Dork.

"—music—"

Ms. Lee nodded at Lindsay, who was wearing a T-shirt she'd obviously gotten at the Martha Flynn concert over the summer. Lindsay beamed.

"—or fashion."

Ms. Lee looked at me, and she didn't just nod — she smiled, and the rush of happiness I felt was probably way out of proportion, but oh wow, it was obvious that she knew what I was wearing!

I decided that Ms. Lee was my favorite teacher ever. My favorite PERSON ever.

TEN

SHELLEY HAD A MATHLETE MEETING DURING LUNCH, so she couldn't wait for me to finish talking to Ms. Lee after class. That was okay with me, since it meant I could take my time. I carried my backpack in one hand, not wanting to sling it over my shoulder and squish my hanbok sleeve, and walked up to her desk as the class emptied out. Ms. Lee looked up from a stack of papers and smiled.

"What can I help you with, Chloe?" she said.

I never have trouble asking questions at school, even to the principal, but I'd never asked a teacher if she liked the same music as me before. *Do you listen to Tiger Rabbit too?* suddenly felt like the stupidest question in existence, so I asked my other question instead.

"Can you give me some advice about the family story assignment?"

"Of course." Ms. Lee nodded once, firmly.

"It's my parents," I said, and suddenly I was so

nervous I had to look at the floor and clamp my arms across my stomach.

"I'm not surprised," Ms. Lee said in a semi-laughing way, which made my nerves settle down a little.

"They . . . you remember my 'pseudo-Korean' paper from last year? My parents didn't help me with that at all."

"Hmmm." Ms. Lee stopped smiling. "I remember some of what you wrote about them."

"Yeah, well, it's even worse than that."

I was breaking one of the most important rules of dealing with teachers: NEVER blame your parents for a crappy grade. It's like saying your dog ate your homework—they won't believe you, and you'll be on their suspicious list from then on.

I took a deep breath, and when I breathed out that lungful of air a giant avalanche of frustration came crashing out with it.

"My mom and dad never, ever talk to me about being Korean. They don't tell me anything about when they lived there, or what it was like to come here, or anything else. When I wrote that paper I asked them to help me with it; they just started talking about something else, like I hadn't even said anything!"

Ms. Lee, frowning, put her elbow on her desk and planted her chin on her hand as I got more worked up.

"Shelley and I made mandu the other day and I didn't even bother giving some to my mom because I knew she wouldn't bother to try them. I know the family story assignment is an easy one, but I'm not going to have any family stories, and it's not fair! They won't help me!"

I stopped to take a breath and also realized I was about to cry, so I ended up taking about twenty really deep breaths in a row, which made me dizzy. Ms. Lee just sat there with her chin on her hand until I stopped acting like I needed an ambulance and was able to breathe normally again.

"Sorry," I said, pressing both palms against my forehead. "Sorry for yelling, I . . ."

"It's fine, Chloe." Ms. Lee folded her arms on the desk in front of her. "It sounds like you've been bottling up a lot of frustration."

"Yeah." Understatement of the year.

"I'm glad you're being honest with me," Ms. Lee said. "I want to help you as much as I can, and we can definitely think about how to approach the academic work, but it also sounds like there are other, more personal issues involved. I really encourage you to make an appointment with Mrs. Fenwick — she's the best person to ask for help with family matters."

Aaaaagh, Ms. Lee was sending me to the guidance

counselor! She half-smiled, curling up one side of her mouth.

"Don't look like that, Chloe, I'm not kicking you to the curb—like I said on the first day of class, I understand what it's like being the child of immigrants. We'll talk, and I can help you figure out some strategies for future work. But my guess is that you need to talk to someone about your parents outside of this one assignment, and I'm not the appropriate person for that. Mrs. Fenwick knows how to help you. Okay?"

I heaved a sigh. "Should I go over there right now?"

"I think it can wait a few minutes," Ms. Lee said. "First let's talk about the Model UN project. You know that the family narrative portion of *that* is optional, right?"

I blinked. "It's for extra credit, right?"

Ms. Lee smiled for real, using both sides of her mouth and everything.

"Extra credit *is* optional."

I just stared at her, because even my favorite teacher ever was capable of being completely wrong. Extra credit? *Optional?* Ms. Lee laughed.

"I understand your commitment to getting the extra credit, Chloe, really I do, but I think concentrating on the heart of the project is a good idea, whether you pursue the extra credit or not. I imagine you're pairing up with Shelley for the diplomatic relations part?"

I nodded. "She's France."

"Wonderful. And was I right when I guessed you'd like to explore fashion as another part of the project?"

"Maybe, although I was wondering if it'd be okay to do music instead."

"K-pop? You're obviously a Tiger Rabbit fan."

BAM, just like that I was cheered up.

"Is that . . ." I pointed at Ms. Lee's finger, and she actually blushed a little.

"Yes, that's a Tiger Rabbit ring, although I wear it mostly because it was a gift."

Another Tiger Rabbit fan! I instantly forgave her for the guidance counselor thing.

"It's fine with me if you want to include a popular music element in your project, as long as it ties in to the overall concept of international citizenship. How has K-pop changed South Korea's relationship with the rest of the world, its place in global commerce, its influence on culture?"

"What about its effect on fashion? See, I could combine both things that way!"

"You could, you definitely could, although don't bite off more than you can chew. In the meantime . . ."

Ms. Lee looked at her watch. ". . . you still have time to talk with Mrs. Fenwick and eat your lunch."

I sighed. "Yeah, okay. Can I . . ."

"Check in with me after you talk to Mrs. Fenwick?" Ms. Lee said with a smile. "Of course."

"Thanks."

I left Ms. Lee's classroom and headed for Mrs. Fenwick's office, aka The Least Fun Office in School.

ELEVEN

I STOPPED AT MY LOCKER TO VISIT MY AWESOME violin, then hurried over to Mrs. Fenwick's office. I'd been there once before, just to keep Shelley company when her dad was sick and her grades went down a little.

Mrs. Fenwick's door was open, but I knocked on it anyway. She was at her desk with the contents of a manila folder spread open in front of her.

"Come in, please," she said, sweeping the papers together and tucking them back into the folder like she was doing a magic trick. "You're Chloe, right?"

"Yes," I said. I was used to teachers knowing who I am.

"Have a seat, please," Mrs. Fenwick said, waving at the chair across the desk from her with one hand, and putting the file into her desk drawer with the other. As I sat down she folded her hands on the desk in front of her, looked at my hanbok, and surprised me by not saying anything about it. "What can I help you with, Chloe?"

Awkward. How do you tell a teacher that your mom and dad won't help you with your homework? Especially when the teacher's a guidance counselor and you're pretty sure she won't be able to do anything about it since she has no idea how good your parents are at dodging conversations?

"Um . . ."

Mrs. Fenwick just looked at me, all patient and friendly in a total look-at-me-being-patient-and-friendly way.

"It's my parents," I said. After telling Ms. Lee it actually felt easier to tell someone else, even the guidance counselor. Still not any fun, but easier.

"It often is," Mrs. Fenwick said. "Can you tell me more?"

I told her about the assignment and my problem with getting Mom and Dad to help. She nodded a few times, but mostly she just listened with a very calm expression. I didn't get all mad like when I told Ms. Lee, but I said just about all the same stuff. Maybe telling teachers about your parent problems is like playing the violin—it gets easier with practice. My brain still felt tired when I was done, though.

"Thanks for sharing all of that with me," Mrs. Fenwick said. "I'm sorry you have to contend with this situation. It sounds very difficult."

"Yeah, it is," I said. "How do I get them to help me?"

"Does your grade depend on getting their help?"

Aw, just when she was starting to get on my good side.

"Yes."

Mrs. Fenwick nodded.

"I respect your scholarly ambition, of course," she said. "We can certainly use as many students like you as we can find. However, it sounds like you and your parents are facing bigger issues than one assignment, and I think that's the priority here. I can talk to Ms. Lee about the assignment."

Oh, sure. Apparently "guidance counselor" didn't just mean Least Fun Office in the Entire School, but also Most Useless Office in the Entire School.

"I don't use loopholes," I said, pretending my eyes had been turned into laser beams and I was using them to burn a hole through her forehead and into her brain.

"That's admirable, but I'm sure there's another option."

"There isn't," I said. There probably was, of course, but you don't lower your standards just because the guidance counselor says you can.

"Chloe, just give it some consideration."

"Um . . . okay." What do you say when a teacher (or a guidance counselor) just doesn't get it? "I bet your grades in school weren't as good as mine" isn't really an option . . . "Why don't I draw you a map" probably wouldn't fly either . . .

"Can I ask you a question?" Mrs. Fenwick said. I tensed up, because usually when people say that it means they're about to ask donkey-brained questions about where I'm "really" from or is it true Korean people eat dogs and stuff like that.

"How do you feel about being the only Korean student at George Matthew?"

Whoa, that came out of nowhere — a question that I could actually give a real answer to! I was so surprised that I forgot to be tense.

"Lonely, I guess."

Mrs. Fenwick leaned her elbows on the desk, made one of those bridges between her upright forearms by laying one hand flat on top of the other, and rested her chin on the bridge of hands.

"Makes sense," she said.

"I mean, my best friend is really into all the Korean stuff, and that's great, but she's the only one. And she can't help me with the assignment."

Mrs. Fenwick smiled. "Always back to the

assignment, eh? Chloe, I think it's very good that Ms. Lee is encouraging you to explore your heritage. Try to put your frustrations aside and concentrate on that—you can continue doing this on your own. You don't need their permission."

Well, geez, that was no help at all. I already knew that.

"Do your parents ever say *why* they don't want to talk about Korea?"

"Not really."

"What do you mean, not really?"

"I mean they literally say things like 'It's too hard to talk about Korea,' or 'The past is the past.' Once they just said, 'We're Americans now,' and that was it."

"Okay, let's think about that," Mrs. Fenwick said. "Why do you think it's too hard for them to talk about Korea?"

"I don't know. Maybe they miss it too much or something."

"There are likely to be multiple 'somethings'— keep thinking about that. In the meantime, your family is obviously your best resource for exploring your ancestry, but there are other options. There's a book club at the public library for kids to talk about multicultural books, for example; that might be helpful."

Or not. I like books, but come on.

"There's also a teen support group that meets every weekend at the town cultural center."

Yeah, THAT sounded like a fun way to use my Saturdays. I bet there'd be TONS of Korean kids there! Me and all zero of my new Korean friends could listen to Tiger Rabbit's *Double Bubble Boy Trouble* album and dance, dance, dance!

I opened the door to walk out of Mrs. Fenwick's office, no wiser than when I walked in, and collided with Amanda Kittredge. I had to take one hard step backward to keep from falling down. She'd obviously been listening in at the door, the big sneak. Amanda looked kind of like a squirrel — beady eyes, big bushy ponytail, clutching her purse to her chest.

"Aagh!"

"Oh, hey, Chloe," Amanda said, like we were passing in the hall instead of practically hugging.

"Hey, Amanda, how about NOT falling all over me like a wet blanket?"

"I heard what you said to Mrs. Fenwick," she said, stepping backward into the hall as I closed the door behind me. Amanda's voice was a wild contrast to how she looked. It was low, raspy, and very confident-sounding. She could totally do her own podcast or something.

"Oh, well, that's just peachy," I said, crossing my arms, standing over her. "Eavesdrop much?"

"Have you ever tried one of those DNA genealogy tests?" Amanda said, as if I hadn't said anything at all.

I blinked.

"No. What are they?"

"They're not free, but there are companies that'll take a DNA sample from you and give you information about where your ancestors may have lived over time, and sometimes even the names of specific family members, at least if they've used the same service."

"Huh. No kidding."

"Yeah. It's pretty cool—I found out people in my family lived in Scotland AND Ireland."

I couldn't tell if Amanda was being sarcastic—she's super deadpan. I could tell I was totally jealous that she knew about "people in her family," which obviously meant "people in my family who aren't currently living in the same house with me," or maybe just "people in my family who are dead."

"They got around, huh?"

"Big time," Amanda said, putting a little snark into it. It made me like her a little bit, which annoyed me because it was totally uncool of her to listen in like that.

"You were eavesdropping, you know," I said.

"Yeah, sorry about that," Amanda said, not sounding sorry at all. "I gotta go, I'm Fenwick's next victim. See you."

"Right. Come back alive."

Amanda gave me a deeply ironic thumbs-up, went into Fenwick's office, and shut the door with a click. I stood there for a second, thinking about what she'd said. DNA tests, huh? Talking to Mrs. Fenwick had been a waste of time, but maybe going to her office hadn't been, thanks to sneakypuss Amanda.

TWELVE

On our way to Dad's store we walked past the Hedge Diner, where every kid in school hangs out every weekend since there's nowhere else to hang out, then we passed the florist, and the Primrose Café, where every adult in town hangs out every weekend since there's nowhere else for *them* to hang out.

The first time I went to the Hedge Diner was in third grade. Shelley and I were old enough to sit at a table by ourselves as one of our parents was in the diner with us, but we had no money of our own. Dad took us on a Sunday, which was the one day a week when Aquariums Unlimited was closed. After ordering our grilled sandwiches and milk shakes we banished him to the counter seats, which is where all the parents who weren't actually sitting with their kids went, while we looked for a booth.

"Hi, Eliza!" I said to Eliza Barkley, who was sitting in a booth with Emily Neilson. Shelley gave me a wide-eyed look as we approached the booth, but I ignored her—there were two empty seats in that booth, and Eliza and I had gone to each other's birthday parties every year since preschool. "Look, we have the same watch!"

I took a step back and pointed at my ankle, which had the exact same stripey sock/glittery plastic watch combination on it as Eliza's ankle. They were even the same color, and I grinned happily at Eliza, expecting her to say something about how mutually awesome our taste in fashion was.

Instead, she said "Oh, hi, Chloe," in a voice that sounded like I'd just asked her to clean up a pile of dog poop. She flicked her eyes down at the empty seat next to her, and said "Sorry, you can't sit here, we're waiting for Elizabeth and Tracy."

"Oh. Okay. That's okay, we're just . . . I just wanted to say hi."

"Hi," Eliza said, not looking at me. "I hate it when people are copycats, don't you?" she said to Emily, who looked at me out of the corner of her eye and nodded. I felt like I'd just been kicked in the shin.

"I hate it even more when people are mean," Shelley said in a low voice. Eliza either didn't hear or just pretended not to hear, because she leaned across the table and started talking to Emily in whispers.

"Chloe, let's sit over there." Shelley grabbed my

elbow and pulled, and after a final, hurt look at Eliza I went along.

"HOW much is the GeneGenie thing?" Shelley said, interrupting my car crash on memory lane.

"A hundred dollars," I said, making a lemon-sucking face as I said it. "Or as I like to say, ten dollars more than all the money I have in the entire universe."

"At least you have ninety dollars saved up. I have, like, two dollars right now."

"They do something called mitochondrial sequencing, though. That totally sounds like it's worth a hundred dollars, doesn't it?"

"If you have it, I guess."

"Thus my plan." I rubbed the palms of my hands together as the AQUARIUMS UNLIMITED sign came into view a block ahead.

It wasn't much of a plan, actually, just because we didn't really need one — Dad was always willing to let us work when we wanted to. We might have to scrape algae off of a bunch of slimy tanks, but money was money.

"Chloe! Hey, dream girl!" Darren said as we entered the store. "Hey, Shelley!"

"So gross, Darren," I said. Shelley said hi and

smiled at Darren, clearly not thinking it was gross. "Hi, Dad!"

"Hi, girls, give me just a minute here," Dad said, not looking away from the test tube in his hand. He squeezed an eyedropper into it, and the water turned blue. Darren gave Dad a double thumbs-up.

"Nitrite level normal, sweet!"

"Yes, it's very exciting," Dad said in a robot voice. Darren cracked up. Shelley and I traded looks, very entertained by how funny Darren thought Dad was.

"You girls have a very purposeful look," Dad said, waving for us to follow him up the stairs. "Let me guess, you need money."

"*Work*, Dad, we need work," I corrected him. He smiled at us over his shoulder as he dumped the test tube into the big work sink at the side of the room. The constant bubbling and sloshing in the roomful of aquariums had its usual soothing effect on me.

"Both of you?"

"Yes, please!" Shelley said.

"Okay then. I need to scrub algae from a bunch of the tanks, and the plants in the display tank really need trimming."

"I'll trim plants!" Shelley and I said at the same time.

"The winner," Dad said, pointing at Shelley.

"Wait, we said it at the same time!" I said. Shelley didn't rub it in, but she also went right down to the office to stow her backpack.

"DAD." I put my fists on my hips and glared at Dad, but then he did the same thing, sticking his hip out to the side like I did, which looked super goofy. I cracked up.

"Come on, I'll help you for a little bit," he said, kissing me on the head. "You can tell me about your day."

I did tell him about my day, leaving out the parts that were too hard for moms and dads to hear without freaking out, as we went past Shelley to the rack with all the catfish and loaches. He nodded and asked a few questions, as he usually does, seeming especially curious about Ms. Lee.

"You really like her," he said, scraping a big swatch of algae off the back of the tank of albino cory catfish.

"She's so awesome!" I said. "I feel like I can talk to her about anything, especially about being Korean! She's actually been to Korea, you know."

"Hmm," Dad said, setting a bucket on the floor under the loach tank.

"She's really helping me with my Model UN project."

"That's great, sweetie." Was that a frown? THAT

WAS A FROWN! I decided to unleash my biggest hound.

"I thought maybe I'd ask if I could interview her husband for my project."

It took a second for that to sink in.

"Interview who?" Dad was netting a sick loach, and he fumbled the net for a second. The loach swam out, and he had to corner it with the net a second time.

"Ms. Lee's husband. Er . . . Mr. Lee."

"I doubt very much she'd say yes to that," Dad said, plopping the netted loach into a small plastic container of water that hung on the edge of the bigger loach tank. "Seems inappropriate to bring her family members into the classroom like that."

"What choice do I have?" Saying that, I didn't have to exaggerate my frustration at all. "I'm the delegate from South Korea, and how many other Korean people are there around here?"

I leaned back so I could look past Dad's back and see Shelley. She was looking over one shoulder, and she raised a handful of wet, brown stems and leaves to give me a thumbs-up. She quickly plunged the hand back into the tank and looked down as Dad silently turned and went to the utility sink with the bucket. He filled it with water, staring into it the whole time, grabbed a siphoning tube off the wall, and came back to the loach tank next to me. He propped the bucket of water on a higher shelf, started siphoning the fresh water into the loach tank, and finally turned and looked at me with his arms crossed.

"Okay," he said.

"Okay what?" I finished scraping algae from my tank of plecostomus catfish and put the scraper thing on my tank's plastic side-hanging container.

"I think Darren can handle things here for a half hour or so. Once I'm done with this tank let's take a walk and I'll tell you a story."

I couldn't believe my ears.

"A story about . . . ?" I leaned toward him, cupping a hand behind my ear.

"Just let me finish with this," Dad said, walking to the top of the stairs. "DARREN!"

Dad thumped down the stairs and talked to Darren for a minute, but I didn't hear what they were saying because I was too busy pumping my arms in the air and doing a synchronized jumping-up-and-down thing with Shelley. We only did three jumps, though, and went back to playing it cool when we heard Dad come back.

"Shelley, how about you go on to cleaning tanks when you're done with the plants—that okay with you?" he said as he waved me to come with him.

"Sure thing, Mr. Cho! Darren can help me!"

I felt a small pang at the thought of not getting paid the same amount as Shelley, but it went away when Dad actually walked out of the store, giving me a come-on gesture when I hesitated.

I followed him out, and we walked to a little park two blocks away from the store. It wasn't much of a park, just grass, a few trees, and a couple of benches, but there was a hummingbird and some butterflies flying around, and anyway, I was so amped up that I'd have been fine sitting next to a Dumpster in a parking lot.

Dad took a deep breath, and I mentally stomped on the urge to pelt him with questions.

"Okay," he finally said. "This is a story about your great-uncle."

!!!

THIRTEEN

THE STORY WAS AMAZING. IT TOOK DAD MAYBE fifteen minutes to tell it, and I listened really hard the whole time as butterflies wafted around us and the sun shone down through the trees. The contrast with the story itself was intense.

"I can't believe he escaped from a labor camp," I said, staring at Dad with my mouth open. "I thought that kind of stuff only happened in, like, Nazi Germany."

Dad rubbed the back of his neck with one hand. He looked frowny and uncomfortable, and was talking in a hesitant, stumbling way.

"No, it still happens in North Korea," he said without looking at me.

"Did you and Mom ever go there? North Korea, I mean?" I said.

Dad shook his head.

"We had . . . my . . . no. I was just a baby when

we lived in Seoul," he said, kind of mumbling. "So was your mother."

"So wait, I thought you were older than that when you came here? Your mom and dad died in a car crash, and you were adopted by —"

"We should get back," Dad said.

"But can you just tell —"

Dad tapped his watch with one finger and got up from the bench.

"There are some calls I need to make, and I should check up on Shelley."

Oh right, Shelley, who I'd totally forgotten about. I felt a pang of guilt, then decided she was getting paid for her time, so why feel guilty? Dad was telling family stories, finally!!!

"Dad, what else —"

"How are you doing with that violin, by the way?" he said, walking back to the store at a much faster pace than we'd taken on the way to the park.

"My . . . my violin? It's great, I love it. It's the best. I just wanted to ask if —"

But dang, we were already back at the store. I realized I'd actually been *jogging* to keep up with Dad's superfast walking speed. Dad opened the door, and we walked into the middle of a small crowd of people, all of them talking at once. Darren looked at Dad with an unmistakable expression of relief.

"Mr. Cho, these people are from the Primrose Aquarist Club, they —"

"We have some questions for you, Mr. Chang!" one wrinkled old lady said.

Ack. I clenched my fists.

"It's CHO," I said in a loud voice, but the old aquarium people were even louder. Dad quickly kissed me on the head.

"Darren, I'll take over here — can you make sure Chloe and Shelley get paid?"

"No problem, Mr. Cho. Okay, Chloe, did you actually work at all today?"

"Well, yeah, a little . . . So an hour for Shelley . . ."

I gave Darren the details as Dad raised a hand and was swallowed up by the mob.

"Yes, yes, I'm happy to answer any questions, no, ma'am, we don't carry that, yes, we should have that by . . ."

My usual irritation was overruled by my excitement about being paid and hearing an actual family story from Dad, so instead of punching anyone in the kneecaps I weaved and shoved through the crowd and went upstairs. Shelley was sitting on an overturned bucket, scribbling something in a notepad, and she looked up fast with a guilty expression, but relaxed when she saw it was me.

"So?" Shelley said, standing up.

I grinned as I took her hand and socked a ten-dollar bill into it.

"Awesome, but I meant your dad."

I kept grinning and waggled my eyebrows for emphasis.

"He told you something good, didn't he?" Her eyes went wide.

I nodded.

Shelley squealed, and we jumped up and down again, not even caring if any of the aquarium club people were watching. For the first time EVER, I actually knew something about my family history. Just as important, I was totally getting an A on the first assignment of the year.

FOURTEEN

THE NEXT WEEK I GOT ANOTHER FUN SURPRISE—
the DNA testing kit from GeneGenie.com. Mom had
picked up the mail on the way out of the house for a
late meeting, and she left it in a pile on the kitchen
table when she got back late, so I didn't find the kit
until I dug through the pile before breakfast the next
day. I hurriedly stuffed the kit into my backpack,
hoovered up my waffles and ham, then ran to
Shelley's house as fast as I could.

I never thought much about the rest of our family
when I was really little—Mom and Dad told me my
grandparents died before I was born, and that neither
of them had any brothers or sisters, which was why I
didn't have any cousins, and that was it. It was during
a playdate in second grade when I noticed one of the
big differences between my house and Shelley's house.
I don't remember it that clearly, because you know,
second grade.

"Who's that lady?" I remember asking, pointing at a framed picture on top of Shelley's dresser.

"My grammy," Shelley said. "Want to play Porcupine Fairies?"

I did, and I forgot about the picture of Shelley's grammy until the next time I came over, and the time after that, and the time after that. Grandparents, aunts, uncles, cousins — Shelley's house was FULL of family pictures. Our house didn't have any.

Dang it, I wanted some pictures.

"Wow, perfect timing," Shelley said as I tore open the package from GeneGenie right there on her front porch. The contents weren't much to look at — a giant Q-tip sealed in plastic, a plastic collection tube, a pre-addressed envelope that looked like it could survive a nuclear holocaust, and a couple of forms to fill out. Shelley and I leaned our heads together as we read the instructions and tried not to spill the entire kit on the ground.

"That's it, huh?" Shelley scratched her head. "Just rub the swab on the inside of your cheek and mail it in?"

"Well, I have to send in all of the money I made working at the store this week."

"Yeah, but you don't have to draw blood or anything like that, right?"

"I guess not," I said. "Not very dramatic. Well, here goes."

I used the swab to scrape the inside of my cheek — it felt a little bit like brushing my teeth with a really soft toothbrush, except on my cheek instead of my teeth. I stuck the swab into the plastic canister, screwed the top on, and stuck it all in the indestructible envelope.

I inspected the form, which had a whole bunch of stuff I couldn't understand. There was also a pair of lines that made me pause.

> You must be 18 years of age to submit a DNA sample to GeneGenie.com.
>
> Your age:

Well now. How badly did I want to know? Enough to lie about my age?

Yes.

I flattened the form against Shelley's front door, wrote *18* for my age, then scrawled my signature across the bottom.

"You know what would be freaky?" Shelley said

"What?"

"If you did one of these and found out you have family members you've never met."

I nodded.

"That's what I'm hoping to find out!"

We went two blocks out of our way to drop the package into a mailbox, then hurried off to school, where we were allowed to use the whole social studies period to work on our projects. Shelley and I decided to focus on researching the cultural history thing for our own countries so we could do a compare-and-contrast thing with our fake diplomatic identities. We had a ton of notes, a ton of printouts, and a total of fourteen books piled on our desks, and as we plowed through all of it Ms. Lee walked around the room, handing back our primary source assignment.

I'm never nervous about grades, not ever, so it was a shock to realize how jittery I was about getting my assignment back. It was the first time I'd ever turned in something that was completely based on stuff my parents told me (even if it was just Dad), and my palms were really sweaty by the time Ms. Lee put my paper facedown on my desk. I looked up at her hopefully, but she was already moving toward another part of the room.

Shelley was furiously scribbling something down out

of a book as I turned the paper over. I was nervous, like I said, but I also had my usual tingle of anticipation about seeing a nice, pointy little A at the top of the page. Instead I saw this:

F—please see me after class

Everything in the room suddenly looked ten feet farther away, and all the sound in the room got fuzzy and muffled, like I'd just dunked my head in a tub of cotton candy. My heart started thumping like crazy, and the edges of the paper crinkled as I squished them even harder with my clammy hands.

An F? An *F??* WHY?? And not even a "Chloe" at the end of the note, just "see me after class," like I was some anonymous pukeface who hadn't been getting straight As her entire life! I must have made some kind of sound—a snarl, or, I don't know, maybe a whimper—because Shelly looked up with a concerned expression on her face.

"What?" she said. I wordlessly held up the paper in her direction as I looked at Ms. Lee, feeling like my eyes were about to pop out of my head. I couldn't catch Ms. Lee's eye at first—she was looking in the opposite direction—but she turned around and saw me, looking too pathetic to ignore, I guess. She handed back one more paper and came over to my desk.

"Are you okay, Chloe?" she said, sounding like she

actually meant it even though she'd just stuck a knife between my ribs.

"NO," I said. Everyone was talking, and not quietly, but a few heads still turned in my direction. I held up the paper. Looking at the bright red F on it was as painful as if she'd carved it into my arm.

"How would I be okay? Why . . . how . . ."

My brain got jammed up, and I might have started drooling. *I'd never gotten an F before*. Fs were for OTHER people.

Ms. Lee held up one hand, looking calm but firm.

"I want to talk about it, Chloe, I do. I know this isn't typical for you. After class."

"But I did the assignment! My dad——"

"Chloe. After class." Ms. Lee's stare wasn't mean or angry, but it definitely was all business. We locked eyes, and was I gonna let her stare me down when she was being so unfair? No way!

"*Chloe,*" Ms. Lee said, and I realized she wasn't backing down either.

"Fine," I said. "I just——"

"We'll work it out, Chloe."

With any other teacher I would have just been mad, but this was Ms. Lee, and that made it hurt too. I finally looked down when I could tell I was about to start crying. I dropped the mangled report, rubbed my hands on my legs, and clenched my entire body into a single, giant knot of muscle until the about-to-cry feeling went away.

I felt a hand on my shoulder and looked up to see Shelley with her arm stretched out between our desks.

"NO. WAY." Her eyes were almost perfectly round. "How could she—"

"I don't know."

"Your dad told you all that stuff!"

"I know."

Everything in that assignment came straight from my dad! How could Ms. Lee give me an F for reporting on my family's actual history??

FIFTEEN

SHELLEY AND I GOT A LOT OF STUFF DONE DURING the rest of class even though I was totally messed up by Ms. Lee stabbing me in the back. South Korea and France turned out to have an interesting history together, which almost (but didn't) stop me from thinking about the F for the entire time. I was so mad that at one point I actually spelled my own name wrong.

It was hard not to throw dagger-eyes at all the kids who were talking about video games, sports, or clothes instead of doing work. Normally I wouldn't hesitate — Mom always says the sharpest knife in a person's drawer is an A, and I've always had the sharpest knives in school — but suddenly I was the one packing a lousy butter knife of an F.

The last bell finally rang, triggering the usual stampede to the cafeteria.

Shelley mouthed "SO UNFAIR" as she got up from her desk, making sure she was facing away from Ms. Lee. I nodded, grinding my teeth as Shelley walked out and left me alone with Ms. Backstabbing F-Giver. Ms. Lee closed the door and smiled at me, which made no sense at all since she was such a traitor to straight-A students everywhere. She grabbed a book off of her desk and, surprisingly, dragged a chair over to my desk.

"Chloe—"

"HOW COULD YOU GIVE ME AN F??" I couldn't hold it in any longer.

Ms. Lee frowned as she sat down.

"Calm down, Chloe. I know you're upset, but you need to control yourself."

"But . . . this is . . ."

"Hey." Ms. Lee put one hand flat on top of my stack of library books. "You'll get to tell your side of the story, Chloe, but first you need to listen to me."

I clenched my fist, then crossed my arms, then clenched my shoulders. Ms. Lee waited until I stopped twitching and clenching.

"Ready?" she said when I could finally sit still.

"Go ahead." I threw my head back and tried to make my face as blank as possible.

"I want to explain this and hear you out because even after such a short time together it's clear you're an exceptional student," Ms. Lee said. "May I?"

She pointed at my now-raggedy paper. I nodded, and she picked it up.

"This is a very compelling story, but I know it's not about your uncle. Every detail in this paper comes from a book called *Flight from Camp 22* that was published a few years ago.

"This is plagiarism, Chloe."

Plagiarism? *Plagiarism??* I opened my mouth, but all that came out was a strangled hiss.

"I know how much trouble you've been having getting help from your parents, Chloe, but this isn't the solution."

"But I didn't do it!" Oh, my head was going to explode. "I would NEVER do that!"

Ms. Lee flipped open my report to the second page, then put the book in her hand in front of me. *Flight from Camp 22* was spelled out in red letters on a white background, with a barbed-wire design (also red) surrounding it. Under the title was a picture of a Korean man, younger than my dad, with a shaggy mess of hair and a mysterious expression.

"I've noted some of the details that match what's in the book."

Ms. Lee held out my report, open to the second page, and I looked at it, not wanting to and really wanting to at the same time. There was a red circle around the words "Camp 22," as well as a bunch of others.

"You can read the book if you'd like to confirm it

for yourself, but this can't possibly be an accident. I would have preferred a blank report over plagiarism, Chloe. I don't know what else to say."

"My DAD told me that story! I didn't copy it out of anything, I've never even heard of this book before!"

Ms. Lee leaned back in her chair and sighed.

"Chloe, you can't blame . . ."

"It's the truth!"

Ms. Lee frowned. We sat without talking for a minute, with her obviously thinking about it, and me digging my fingernails into my palms. She'd practically called me a liar, and it was getting hard to keep myself from totally losing it when she finally spoke again.

"I think we need to arrange a conference with your father."

I exhaled, only then realizing that I'd been holding my breath.

"I think so too."

Then it hit me. *I* wasn't a cheater. *I* wasn't a liar.

But maybe Dad was.

SIXTEEN

I hit Aquariums Unlimited like a computer-guided missile, blasting through the doors and scanning the front room with one target in mind.

"Whoa, Chloe, what's going—"

I cut off Darren with a violent wave of my arm.

"Where's my dad?"

Darren was paused in mid-motion, one hand holding a box of filter cartridges and the other holding a bag with a big, scaly catfish in it. The customer at the counter, who I didn't recognize, stared at me over his shoulder.

"In the back with a customer." Darren waved the box of filter cartridges in that direction. "Chloe, you gotta watch it with that door, it'll—"

"Thanks."

I clomped up the stairs two at a time. Dad was pointing at a tank as he explained something to Lindsay Crisp's sister Danielle, who was a senior in high school. She looked at me like I was a mosquito and immediately looked away, but it was enough to make Dad switch his attention from her to me.

"Hi, honey, can you wait for me downstairs? I'm right in—"

"I got an F on my paper, Dad. The one about my uncle, who I guess isn't real."

Dad shut his mouth with a click—I actually heard his teeth snap together.

"Your story about my great-uncle came from a BOOK. You LIED to me! Why did you LIE? I GOT AN F!!"

"I'm sorry, Danielle, this is—Darren will have to take over for me," Dad said without looking at her.

"Oh, I can wait," Danielle said, suddenly looking at me like I was the most interesting thing she'd ever seen. Of course. *Asian honor student gets kicked out of the straight-A club! Fascinating!*

"Darren will help you," Dad said. "Darren? Can you come up here and help Danielle?"

"Sure thing," said Darren's voice from somewhere downstairs. His feet came thumping up the stairs. Danielle stared at us like we were giving a live performance just for her. Dad weaved between me and her, around the big tank of plants, and down the stairs, with me right behind him. Darren gave Dad a curious look and me a quick smile as we passed each other.

The downstairs office was the size of a toaster oven, but at least it had a door. I closed it behind me as Dad sank into his chair, which was squeezed in front of his desk. There were as many boxes in the office as there were in the storage room, including a giant pile on top of the only other chair in the room, so I stood with my back to the door. I didn't feel like sitting down anyway.

Dad took a deep breath.

"Honey, I . . . I'm . . ."

"I can't believe you pretended something you read from a book was about our family! That's what you did, right?"

Dad's mouth was still open, but instead of saying anything he made it into an "O" shape and blew out a long breath. He dragged a hand all the way down his face, forehead to chin.

"Yes."

"You're a liar, Dad. A LIAR!"

"I'm . . . I'm sorry, sweetie. How did you find out?"

"I told you, I got an F on my paper. Ms. Lee knows that book."

"I'm . . . I'm honestly surprised anyone in Primrose Heights would be interested in a book on North Korea."

"Ms. Lee is. She's KOREAN and everything, you know."

"Yes, I know. I just didn't . . . I know."

"Do I even have a great-uncle named Ho-Joon?" I said. "Or any kind of uncles at all? What else about my life is made up? All of it?"

Dad put both hands on top of his head.

"I guess it's time to tell you the truth."

"Oh, do you think?"

Dad looked pained by my sarcastic tone.

"Yes."

"About EVERYTHING," I said. Except I didn't know if I wanted to know about everything, because what if it actually was everything, and not just this one thing? What if it was my whole life??

I put my hands over my face and rubbed it hard, squishing my nose and mashing lips against my teeth.

"Yes, yes, about everything, I promise, but not without your mother. We need to tell you together."

"Why can't you tell me right now??"

"You need to hear it from both of us, honey." Dad dropped his hands and looked me in the eye — not in a mad way, in more like an I'm-saying-please kind of way. "Your mom doesn't have class so she's probably home right now. Let me tell Darren what's happening and we'll go together."

I gulped in a lungful of air and blew it out. "Fine."

The drive home is stupidly short — three minutes,

tops—but I was so mad, worried, and confused, it felt like it took a day and a half. When Dad pulled into the driveway and killed the engine I scrambled out, slammed the car door hard, and ran inside before he'd even opened his door all the way.

"Mom!" I called. I shoved the front door open hard, but caught it before it hit the wall out of habit. I threw my backpack against the wall with a thump. "MOM!"

"Hi, hello, I'm here, what is it, Chloe?" Mom emerged from the kitchen with a coffee cup and a magazine. "Why are you shouting?"

"I'm not shouting," I said, lowering my voice.

The report was still in my hand—I'd held it all the way to the store, then all the way home, so the sweat stains on the edges were out of control—and I stuck it out in Mom's direction, F side up.

"Oh dear," she said in a low voice, taking it from me. "Oh, Chloe, this is . . ."

She trailed off as she started reading the actual paper, and when Dad opened the door she looked up at him with such an angry expression that I forgot about the F for a second and wondered why she was mad at HIM. Were we living in Bizarro World?

"What is going on?" Mom said, not using a low voice anymore.

Dad, shockingly, looked mad too. He doesn't raise his voice when he's mad, but he started talking more slowly, with a little bit of a growl, as he shut the front door and stood next to me.

"What's going on is we're telling Chloe the truth."

"What do you mean the truth, about . . ."

Mom and Dad locked eyes, and not in a gross, lovey-dovey way — they looked like a couple of kickboxers getting ready to beat each other up. It was a little scary.

"What did you do?" It was Mom's turn to crush the edges of my paper in her hands.

"We should have told her a long time ago, and you know it." Dad crossed his arms, and Mom started talking in a really fast voice I'd never heard her use before.

"I can't believe you thought it would be okay to make this decision on your—"

Why were Mom and Dad fighting? Especially now? Why did they only care about themselves??

"STOP!" I shrieked, clamping my hands on top of my head. I could actually smell the sweat on them — the entire world smelled like sweat and fish water and bad feelings. "STOP FIGHTING, STOP STOP STOP!"

They actually did stop. It was a miracle. I felt weird standing next to Dad, like I was taking his side against Mom or something, so I stepped right in between them. My heart was like a giant rabbit thumping the ground with its foot as I ripped the paper out of Mom's hands—most of it, anyway; she was left holding a torn-off page. I spun around, almost crashing into Dad, went to the living room, and sat down on the overstuffed armchair facing the couch.

My heart slowed down a little, but I still felt like my insides were being run through a food processor as Mom and Dad followed me into the living room and sat on the couch. They sat next to each other, which was a relief after the intense staring, but we were all tense. Which was so confusing, because *I* was the one being lied to!

Mom was still giving Dad a very harsh look, though, and he could have been a robot, his face was so empty-looking. Since she was too busy looking at Dad to look at me, I looked at him too.

"Well? You're both here, like you said it had to be. So tell me."

"Now listen, Chloe—" Mom started, but nuh-uh, it wasn't gonna happen that way.

"Don't give me NOW LISTEN CHLOE, just tell me why Dad stole something out of a book and told me it was about our family!"

Mom hissed, like a serious snakelike hiss, and Dad frowned at her.

"We knew this was going to happen," he said to her. "It was only a matter of time."

Mom started rubbing her temples. "Yes, I know, but of all the stupid—"

"We've both been stupid."

"It's just so maddening that you would engage in such blatant plagiarism when your wife is a *college professor*," Mom said, putting all of her fingertips on her temples.

"HEY." Not this again. "MOM. DAD. What is going on? I got an F!"

"That's my fault, and I apologize," Dad said.

Awesome! Your apology will bring my grade all the way up from an F to an F!

"Yeah, well, Ms. Lee wants to talk to you about it."

"Forget about that right now." Dad looked at Mom one more time. "Are you with me right now? Our daughter needs us, *right now*."

Mom pressed her lips together, but she also nodded slowly.

"This isn't how it should happen," she said.

"This is how it IS happening."

"It's how what's happening??" I threw my hands up in the air. "What, what, WHAT?"

"Honey, we're not Korean," Mom said.

I let my hands fall onto the armrests of my chair

with a double THUMP. I could have sworn Mom said "We're not Korean," but why would she say that??

"Okay . . . that's a pretty weird thing to say."

Dad ran a hand through his hair.

"It's true, sweetie," he said.

"What are we, then, Chinese? German? Werewolves?"

"Not werewolves," Mom said, and geez, she just kept right on saying the last thing I expected her to say.

"We're not Korean," Dad repeated. "We're not even from Earth. Your mother and I were born and raised on an Earth-like planet in the Tau Ceti solar system, and we came here after . . . I guess you could call it a natural disaster."

Dad paused.

"We're aliens," he said.

"And so are you," Mom added.

SEVENTEEN

Okay, I was wrong about the werewolf comment being the most unexpected thing they could say. Dad had just taken it to another level.

Oh my god, they're insane. My parents are mentally ill.

Everyone I know says their parents are insane sometimes, and yeah, it's mean to both parents and real insane people to say it, but nobody really means it. But then your parents tell you you're actually an alien from another planet, and you realize you've stumbled into a moment when your parents might actually be totally legit, locked-up-in-the-attic crazy.

Not a good moment.

"Wait, what? You're what, I'm what??"

Mom took a deep breath.

"You were born here on Earth, but you're an alien too."

Dad, wearing his supercalm face, adjusted his alien butt on the couch and leaned forward.

"We know this is hard to believe, honey." He held

his hands out in front of his belly, palms down and fingers spread.

"OH, YOU THINK?"

"That's one reason why we waited so long to tell you, sweetheart," Mom said. I could tell she was worried about me, but I was really distracted by fear about her mental health.

"Mom . . ." I sagged all over, all at once. "This is . . . you're talking like a crazy person. There's no such thing as real aliens."

"I know it's hard to believe. I know. But it's the truth."

I looked back and forth between Mom and Dad, wondering if my head was going to explode.

"Why are you saying this? Are you trying to teach me some kind of weird lesson?"

"No, honey," Dad said. "We're being honest with—"

"No you're not. I'm not a stupid little baby that just believes anything you say, you know. I'm an ALIEN? How is that being honest??"

Mom and Dad looked at each other, both of them with an oh-that's-just-great kind of look on their faces, and I felt scared again, but in a different way. They actually believed what they were saying—I can always tell when they're lying. Were they losing their minds for real?

What was I supposed to do if my parents were mentally ill?

I scrubbed my scalp with all ten fingers and gulped.

"We'll show you," Mom said. "We can prove it. Or I should say, your dad can prove it to you."

She glared at Dad, and he looked back with his eyebrows raised.

"You know it always affects me more than it affects you, and I need to be functional tomorrow," Mom said.

Dad nodded.

"Okay, sure. You're right, I always did recover more quickly than you. Come on, Chloe."

"How are you going to prove something that's not real, Dad?" *Or that's a sign of you being crazy?* "Are you introducing me to Uncle Ho-Joon from North Korean Labor Camp Twenty-Two?"

"No. It's in the greenhouse—in the aquaponic tank."

"I'll get the vinegar," Mom said, heading for the kitchen.

"The *what*? Why do we need—"

"We'll show you." Dad didn't wait for Mom—he went straight through the house, opened the sliding glass door at the back, and went out into the yard.

I didn't even know Mom knew where the vinegar was. I didn't even know she knew *what* vinegar was.

I was getting really, really scared.

It was normally my favorite time of day during my favorite time of year — it was still warm and the sun wasn't setting yet, but it was low enough in the sky to make those long, really pretty shadows through the trees. Being out there settled me down a little bit, and I breathed in the smell of leaves and grass as I followed Dad across the yard.

Dad's greenhouse is right up against the part of the backyard fence opposite from the house — he says if it was up against the house it would make it too hot. I heard the back door of the house open and close behind us as Dad unlocked the greenhouse, and Mom appeared next to me with a bottle of vinegar in her hand. Dad looked over his shoulder as he opened the door and saw the bottle.

"Red wine vinegar? Really?"

"It's all we have."

Dad made a "huff" noise as we followed him into the greenhouse. As usual, walking in there felt kind of like having a very thin, light, damp blanket draped over me. Trickly water sounds came from everywhere, and the smell of leaves and grass from outside was immediately taken over by the smell of water and fish. Something always smelled like fish at the Cho house.

"Dad—"

"Here."

We stood in front of the biggest tub of water and plants, right in the middle of the greenhouse. Dad dipped a hand into it, swirled the water around for a minute, then pulled it back out with a fish in it. It was one of the smaller fish in the tank, about half the size of Dad's hand.

"They look healthy," Mom said in her scientist-at-work voice.

"This is a species that's native to our home world in Tau Ceti," Dad said, holding the wiggly fish up for me to see.

"Dad . . ." This was *not* doing anything to reassure me. "You're not gonna bite its head off or anything like that, are you?"

"I won't hurt it at all—in fact, this can be beneficial for the fish, if not so much for us."

Dad brought the fish up to his face and LICKED IT.

"EEEEWWWW!" I couldn't believe my eyes.

It was a fast, tiny lick—it was almost like Dad poked the fish with his tongue, superfast—but it was still licking a live fish! It was like seeing a terrible accident on the side of the freeway; you know it's bad, but you just have to look.

This day was never going to stop getting weirder.

"Aren't there eighty kinds of bacteria in that water??" I said, meaning normal Earth bacteria. "You're not gonna barf, are you?"

Dad managed to pucker his mouth and lick his lips at the same time. A strange smell started coming from the fish, or was it coming from Dad? Mom must have seen me twitching my nose or something.

"I don't like the smell either," she said with a little bit of a smile. "It goes away quickly, though."

"There's a chemical reaction between our saliva and the fish's mucus coating," Dad said. "It also takes care of the bacteria issue—the water in this tank is different from the water in the rest of the tanks."

"And let me guess, the spit in your mouth is also different from the spit in other people's mouths?"

Dad nodded. "Not a big difference—on a genetic level we're 99.999 percent identical—but the enzyme mix in our saliva is one of the only noticeable differences."

Spit. That was the difference between being human and being alien—spit. Humans rule, aliens drool. I was suddenly more aware of the spit in my mouth than ever before.

"The chemical reaction happens right on the skin of the fish, but its skin has a lot more mucus. When there's more saliva than mucus the air interferes with the reaction, so it needs to happen inside our mouths or on our tongue."

Dad's generous use of the word "mucus" wasn't doing anything for my stomach. He held the fish in front of his chest, and I wondered if it was dying from lack of oxygen.

"Shouldn't you put that back in the water?" I couldn't help worrying about the stupid fish.

"It's fine, it has a reservoir of oxygen inside. Watch, now."

The fish from another planet was glowing where Dad had licked it. The glow was almost like a turquoise color, and when Dad stuck out his tongue, the tip was glowing the same color. There was just a tiny spot of color in both places, but the glow started spreading outward as I watched.

An albatross could have flown into my mouth with room to spare.

"Whoa . . ." I leaned in for a closer look. The fish and Dad's tongue both looked partly transparent, as if the glowing slime-and-spit mix had sunk into their surfaces.

"Oh my god, so freaky. Does . . . does doing that make you sick or something?"

"A little nausea, only because I don't do it very often. The vinegar counteracts it . . ."

Mom handed the vinegar to Dad. He took the bottle and took a swig out of it, blech, and swished it around in his mouth. He spit right into the tank of plants and fish, making me promise myself that I'd never put my hand into that tank unless it was really, really important.

"I know that's unpleasant, but the nutrients can still be used by the fish," Dad said with an apologetic shrug. He put the cap back on the vinegar and folded his arms. Then the three of us spent a hundred years standing there and not looking at each other. Actually, I didn't know if they were looking at me or not, because it was too hard to look at them without thinking . . . strange thoughts.

"Do you believe us now?" Dad's voice was gentle.

"Have you tested it on a normal person?" I said in a wobbly voice.

I let my hand flop down to my side, because I knew what Dad had done just wasn't normal. People's tongues don't light up like glow sticks. Mom put her hand on my shoulder, and I shook it off. Mom left her hand hanging in the air for a second, but I stared at it and not at her, and she slowly pulled it back.

"I have, actually," Dad said. "I know this is all new to you, but it's not new to us—we've spent a lot of time learning about all of it."

I took a deep breath and ran my hands through my hair.

"So what does that . . . do?" I said, my voice shaking a little.

"What do you mean?" Dad said.

"I mean can you, like, read minds or, I don't know, breathe underwater now? Is the fish slime magic?"

Dad smiled a tight, pained-looking smile.

"No, there's no magic. The reaction looks pretty dramatic, but it's purely cosmetic."

"Can I . . . is that something I can do too?"

Dad nodded.

"Do I *need* to do it?" Dad shook his head, and I felt relieved, because if I had to lick a fish to, I don't know, live under the light of a yellow sun or something, I'd basically have to light myself on fire.

That was when I realized I did believe them.

EIGHTEEN

BELIEVING WE WERE A FAMILY OF ALIENS MADE NO sense. We had no antennae! Where were the bug eyes? Our skin wasn't green. Maybe that's why Dad licked the fish slime, though, to keep his skin from turning green! But I'd never had any fish slime. Not that I knew, anyway! WERE MOM AND DAD SECRETLY FEEDING ME FISH SLIME??

I spun on my heel and walked outside. I heard Dad say "Chloe" from behind me as I bolted across the yard. It took me two tries to get a grip on the doorknob, and I made a *NNNNNNGGGGG* sound until I was able to open the door, get inside, and close the door behind me. I slumped back against the door for a minute.

Not Korean. Not even human. Not *me*. Looked like I'd wasted a hundred bucks on that GeneGenie thing — their database probably didn't include people from other solar systems.

I couldn't decide if I wanted to keep moving or stop moving. I stalked back and forth across the living room twice, then stopped and stared at nothing. I heard the back door open and close, and when Mom and Dad came into the living room I blinked at them, kind of wanting to throw something at them and kind of wanting to lie facedown on the floor.

"So we're not Korean at all."

"We should have told you earlier than this," Dad said. Mom gave him an angry look, but managed to wipe the anger off her face before looking back at me.

"We've spent a lot of time talking about it, honey," she said. "We wanted to do the best thing for you."

"Lying to me was the best thing, huh?" I kicked at the carpet, leaving a dirty scuff mark.

"No, it wasn't," Dad said.

"Will you *stop*?" Mom barked it out without even looking at Dad. "You know it's never been that simple!"

"Maybe it is, though," Dad said. "Maybe it always has been. Can we all sit down? Please?"

Mom and Dad sat on the couch with a three-foot gap between them that looked all wrong, and I decided to sit down on the carpet, right where I was standing. Then I decided to flop onto my back and stare at the ceiling, because it was still hard to look at Mom and Dad.

"It is . . . was the fourth planet from the sun in the

Tau Ceti system. Tau Ceti Four. Our home world."
Mom's voice sounded different enough to make me
lift my head off the carpet and look at her. She was
looking down at her hands, and it was a relief to see
Dad reach out and put his hand on her back. I sat all
the way up.

"That's not the most interesting name, I know, but
it's what we call it here on Earth."

"Was?" I said.

"There was a solar event," Dad said. "We don't
know what exactly happened, but the sun . . .
changed. We were forced to leave."

"We were in the equivalent of college," Mom said.
"It was the only reason we were able to escape."

"It was chaos," Dad said. "Nothing was working
the way it was supposed to. We were extremely
lucky that your mom was working in the astrophysics department."

"I was involved with the development of an experi-
mental spacecraft." Mom sounded proud, even though a
tear was leaking out of the corner of her eye. She wiped
it away with the tip of her pinkie. "Your dad and I
were . . ."

"We were looking at your mom's work," Dad said.
"We were in the astrophysics lab when it happened.

We didn't know if the ship would even fly, but it was the only choice we had."

"I knew it would fly." Mom sat up a little straighter.

"So we left, and just in time. The planet . . ."

Dad stopped talking, took a deep breath, and rubbed his chin with one hand. I was listening so hard I could hear his fingers make a raspy, sandpapery sound across his chin stubble.

"So you flew to this planet. In a spaceship."

"Yes."

"And you decided to come to *Primrose Heights*? The most boring place on . . ."

I was going to say "on Earth," ha-ha.

"We were able to do some research," Dad said. "Initially we decided to go to Korea, because of all our physical similarities — it seemed like the best place to blend in. That turned out to be a mistake."

"That doesn't make any sense," I said.

"It was the *hardest* place to blend in, because we so obviously weren't Korean," Mom said. "We did it all wrong, everything from speaking the language to finishing a bowl of noodles. It was very, very uncomfortable."

Mom and Dad traded little smiles, like they were remembering something that was funny and awful at the same time.

"So we decided to come here instead," Mom said. "We've been able to pursue our work and have our family here."

"But . . . but . . . here? You know people in this town don't know anything about being Korean, right?"

"That was the point," Dad said. "People don't know any better here. It matters much less if we accidentally do or say something that reveals our true identities. Sometimes I still say occasional words in our native language, but anyone in Primrose Heights who hears me will assume I'm speaking Korean."

"We're still learning how to function in this world," Mom said. "It helps that every time we make mistakes about being Earthlings, our neighbors all assume they're mistakes about being American."

"What about me, though? Do you know how much stupid crap I have to listen to every day? 'Hey, Chloe, nice kimono, hey, Chloe, I didn't know Oriental girls talk so much, hey, Chloe, you're good at math, right?'"

"Well, you are very good at math," Mom said.

"I don't even know what a geisha girl is, but I know I'm not one of them."

"Er, no, you're definitely not." Dad sighed. "I'm sorry you have to deal with that. That's . . . I'm sorry. The alternative is worse, though."

"What's worse than being surrounded by racists all the time?"

"That might be a little harsh, Chloe . . . The alternative is, well, almost anything. If our secret became known there'd be no shortage of people who'd view us as a threat to global security. At best, we could be the targets of constant harassment. At worst, we could be captured and imprisoned. We *have* to hide our true ancestry."

I had to stop and think about that. Jail. Jail for aliens. Or maybe lab experiments ON aliens, which would at least be kind of interesting, but probably even worse.

On the plus side, this opened up a whole new territory of snappy comebacks. *Abigail Yang's a great violinist, but can she make her tongue glow in the dark? No, I'm not Japanese, you're LIGHT-YEARS off.*

Nobody would believe me, of course. Which I guess was the whole point of coming to our nowhere town, like Dad had said. It actually made sense.

"So . . . we're freaks, then," I said. "We're not Korean, we're not even human. You're saying we're just . . . freaks."

"NO." Mom's expression was fierce. "We are not freaks!"

"But we've just been pretending to be Korean. Well,

YOU'VE been pretending, anyway. I thought it was all real."

"Honey . . ." Dad paused to heave a sigh. "It's true that we're Korean by choice, not by birth—"

"By CHOICE? How can we be Korean by choice? We're not even from this solar system, right?"

I put my hands over my face, then pushed them up into my hair and grabbed a double fistful. If we weren't from Korea, then we didn't have any family members in Korea. Or . . . anywhere?

"Did anyone else get away?" I said in a strangled voice. "From Toe City Four or whatever your planet was called?"

"Tau Ceti Four," Dad said quietly. "And we don't know. There's no way to know."

"What about your . . . I mean our . . ."

I couldn't say it. I just couldn't.

"Our family?" Dad said, and I nodded. He and Mom looked at each other, and suddenly it felt like I was drowning in their sadness. Tears started running down both their faces this time.

"We don't know about them either," Mom said.

"They're dead," I said.

"Probably," Dad said, almost whispering.

I'd never felt every single feeling in the world all at the same time before. My head felt like it would pop like a supercheap balloon. I'd always been so jealous of Shelley for having such a big family. I went to her cousins' house for Easter once, and it was so much fun playing with all of them that I didn't even care when her aunt kept asking me if I was a Buddhist. Well, not much, anyway.

Did I have . . . used to have cousins? I started to ask, but I couldn't do it. I was too afraid to know the answer.

Did *Mom and Dad* have cousins? Not anymore, I guess. They just had me, and I just had them. We were like orphans, right? The most orphaned orphans ever. Well, I wasn't an orphan, but as a family we were like orphans. I decided it was absolutely legit to have a flexible definition of "orphan" if you find out you're from another planet that was destroyed by an exploding sun.

I collapsed all the way onto my back again.

"I can't believe my whole life has just been a fantasy," I said. "I can't believe it."

"Chloe—" Mom said, wiping her eyes, but I interrupted her with a laugh. It might have been more like a screech.

"I mean, at least you're telling me stuff about our real life now. I guess I should be happy, huh?"

"You should feel however you feel," Mom said a few seconds later. "It makes sense that you're upset."

"Upset" was so not the right word. There really wasn't any one word that captured it all; only a phrase would do, like "head in a blender."

"Honey——" Dad said, but I waved him off.

"Don't. Just . . . don't."

Then, because they don't call me Crabby McCrabberCho for nothing, I ran out of the living room and into my room, where I slammed the door, belly-flopped onto the bed, and smashed my pillow on top of my head.

I was an alien from the boringly named planet Tau Ceti Four, in the Tau Ceti galaxy. My life as a normal human being was over—no, it hadn't even existed in the first place. Mom and Dad were so wrong about not being freaks. We were literally the biggest freaks in the world. And I'd thought being Korean in this town was hard! At least I could talk about it, even if Shelley was the only one who cared. What was Shelley going to think about all this?

I yanked the pillow off my head and stared at the wall.

What would Shelley think?

Could I even tell her?

NINETEEN

THE NEXT MORNING DAD LEFT EARLY TO DEAL with a new shipment of fish at the store — at least that's what he said, who knew where he was actually going? Maybe he had to go make crop circles or something. I stared at Mom as I shoveled in my bowl of cereal, wondering what was going on inside her twisted brain. She just smiled and drank her coffee. I scooped up a spoonful of cereal so carelessly that milk sloshed onto my place mat, and that finally got her to react, even if it was just putting her cup down on the table and folding her hands in front of her mouth. I stared at the puddle of milk on my place mat, suddenly feeling sad about it, and the place mat, and the table, and Mom and Dad.

When I left the house I started walking to Shelley's out of habit, but I stopped in mid-step a block away from home. I still had no idea what to say to her — there was no way to tell her the truth without sounding like one of those scary-bizarre newspapers they sell in the supermarket checkout lanes. *Korean Girl Is Actually From Mars!* Or maybe *Legal Alien!* It was your basic unprecedented situation, and after standing there on the sidewalk like a zombie for a couple of minutes, I spun on my heel and walked to school alone.

I stopped at the front doors of the school and looked at all the kids milling around.

Look at all those Earthlings.

I trudged into the building and stopped at the trophy case next to the main office. If you stand at just the right angle you can see your reflection in the glass on the side closest to the front door, and I stared at myself. Kids' faces appeared over my shoulder, some of them looking at me curiously, then were replaced by others. None of those faces looked like mine, of course. None of them ever had. That wasn't anything new—people were always treating me like I was from outer space, and I'd never looked like everyone else, no matter how I acted or what I wore. Were things actually all that different now?

I lifted my hand, palm facing away, and looked at my Tiger Rabbit ring. My favorite K-pop band. Nobody else in Primrose Heights liked K-pop, but nobody else was Korean. K-pop was all mine. Except now it wasn't.

Yeah, it was different. I didn't look like anyone else

in town, but I'd still been *human*. I'd been a Korean human. Now I wasn't anything.

"Hey!" I heard her voice before her reflection appeared in the glass.

"Hey," I said, turning around to face Shelley.

"Where were you? I waited for ten minutes!" Shelley wasn't mad, exactly. It took me a second to figure it out.

Oh great, her feelings are hurt, I thought. *That's just great. Way to go, Space Cadet Cho.*

"I'm sorry, I just . . ." *Found out my parents immigrated from another solar system, not from Korea. You know how it is*. Nope, couldn't say that. ". . . I just had some stuff to do, uh, at the store."

"What store?" Shelley said, for a second looking confused instead of hurt.

"Dad's store."

"Your dad's store isn't open this early." She was getting that hurt look on her face again, but this time it was combined with a mad look. I'd seen Shelley's hurt/mad look before, but it wasn't usually aimed at me. The universe was just determined to throw all kinds of new and interesting experiences at me, I guess.

"I went there with him, we had to . . . It's complicated. I'm sorry I didn't tell you."

"Is there, like, something wrong?" The hurt/mad look vanished, which was terrible because then I felt guilty, and I almost never feel guilty about anything, which made me realize I was totally lying to my best friend, and was something happening to my brain? Did I have alien microbes in my brain? Or maybe I was just tapping into the family talent for lying.

"It's, you know, a fish thing," I said, hoping to throw her off the trail by being vague. "I just had to help my dad because Darren wasn't picking up his phone."

The made-up, Darren-related phone detail did the trick.

"Well, you could have at least answered my texts," Shelley said, but it was her mad-but-forgiving voice. "I have some ideas about the project."

The project. I hadn't even thought about the project since before Mom and Dad tried to crush my sanity with stories about our invaders-from-Mars family history. And poof, just like that I didn't want to work on it anymore.

What a bizarre feeling. I couldn't remember ever not wanting to work on a project before.

". . . when Paris fashions started appearing in Korea, and hellooooo, did you hear anything I just said?"

I twitched and looked at Shelley, blinking, without recognizing her for a second. She stuck her face out so it was just a few inches away from mine.

"Chloe? You there?"

"Sorry, I'm just kind of tired from getting up so early."

"Did you do your—"

The bell rang, which surprised us both. Having to run to class after the bell rings is for people who don't get stuff done, but I guess that was me now, and I was grateful that the bell rescued me from giving Shelley an honest answer to her question, which I knew was going to be *Did you do your diplomatic profile?* Which I hadn't.

I hadn't done an assignment, for the first time in . . . forever?

We bolted to homeroom, got warned for being late, then couldn't talk because of announcements and stuff. It was a strange beginning to what turned out to be a very strange day. I couldn't concentrate on anything—teachers would ask really easy questions, and I'd be, like, the *third* person to raise my hand! A couple of times I couldn't even think of the right answer at all, and the worst was in Earth science, when Mr. Wilson asked, "What is the process by which a gas or liquid moves through a living cell wall?" and I actually said "filtering" instead of "osmosis." I was totally off my game, and it was all Mom and Dad's fault.

By the time social studies rolled around I didn't even care, though. When your whole life is a big lie, literally your WHOLE LIFE, who cares about dissecting frogs and figuring out the volume of a cylinder? I dragged myself into the room and parked my sorry, extraterrestrial butt in my chair. Shelley took her seat a few seconds later.

"Hey, Crabby McCrabberson," she said in a semi-joking voice, still looking tense. "So, about the diplomat profiles —"

I looked at her, and it felt like I was looking from a million miles away, maybe through a really dirty window or something. I felt unplugged from the world. It wasn't like I'd been transformed into a bug-eyed monster or something, but that's what it seemed like.

"I didn't do mine," I said, not even trying to sound like I cared. Shelley obviously cared, though. Her eyes got round, she sucked in her breath, and her fists clenched tightly enough to make her knuckles instantly turn white. I didn't blame her. I hadn't done an assignment, one that impacted *her* grade. If we'd traded places I'd probably be ready to yank her heart right out of her chest.

We hadn't traded places, though, so I just felt guilty

instead. Which was awesome, because if there was anything missing from the rotten garbage sandwich of my life it was a nice thick slice of guilt!

"You . . . you didn't do it?" Shelley said.

"I had a . . . talk with my parents last night. It was intense, and I just . . . I forgot."

"YOU FORGOT?" Shelley didn't yell that part, but she said it loud enough to silence the whole room before Ms. Lee even asked for it.

"Shelley, is everything okay?" Ms. Lee said, looking calm. For a second I remembered how awesome she was, because all of our other teachers (except maybe Mr. C) would have looked all frowny and disrespected, but Ms. Lee looked like she actually had an idea who Shelley was and how barking YOU FORGOT like that wasn't Shelley. Too bad Ms. Lee and I didn't have anything in common anymore. It was like being on one of those talk shows where some sad lady with a baby finds out the baby's dad isn't REALLY the baby's dad, if the baby's dad was, like, a Klingon.

"No . . . I mean, I don't . . . yes, I'm fine, I'm fine." Shelley pressed her lips together, mashed her hands into a ball on her desk, and didn't look at me.

"Are you sure?" Ms. Lee said, still sounding like she actually cared.

Shelley nodded, but she shot me a how-could-you-do-this-to-me look when Ms. Lee turned away. I kind of shrugged, in apology I guess, but it didn't seem to help.

Ms. Lee spent most of the period on, surprise, diplomacy, plus related stuff like treaties, sanctions, and so on. And all I could think about was how all the diplomats on my parents' home planet must be dead. Shelley and I didn't look at each other even once during the whole class, and I caught Ms. Lee looking at us curiously a couple of times.

Finally class was over, and it was time to hand in our diplomatic profiles. Ms. Lee stood at the front of the class, as usual, and accepted the stack of papers from the person at the front of each row of seats. I heard a papery SMACK from the direction of Shelley's desk — probably her slapping her assignment on top of her stack. I took my row's stack of papers without looking behind me and passed it directly into Ms. Lee's hands. She smiled, but with a little bit of a crinkle in her forehead.

"I think you forgot something, Chloe," she said lightly, but with just a touch of question mark at the end.

"No, I didn't," I said, shoveling all of my stuff into

my backpack. "Well, yes, I mean, I did. I forgot to do it."

Ms. Lee frowned.

"Oh. I see. Is there—"

"Sorry," I said, and I slid out of my chair, slung my backpack over my shoulder, and walked out with the rest of the riffraff, feeling very weird about the fact that I was being so . . . I didn't even know what.

Not Korean, maybe.

Shelley caught up with me halfway to the cafeteria.

"Chloe!" she called from behind me. I didn't stop walking until she grabbed my shoulder and forced me to.

"Hey," I said.

"*Hey?*" Shelley put her hands on her hips. "*Hey? You do . . . you do that*"—she flapped her hands wildly behind her, kind of in the direction of Ms. Lee's classroom—"and you just say *hey* like, oh, everything's normal? What is going ON?"

I opened my mouth to tell her, then stood there with my mouth open. I talked to Shelley about everything. It was automatic, you know? So why couldn't I do it now?

"It's . . . complicated."

"Why didn't you do your diplomat profile?" Shelley put her hands on top of her head. "We talked about it for hours—all you had to do was go through your notes and write it up!"

We had spent hours talking about it. It'd been fun, kind of like creating a character for a role-playing game without all the dice and monster manuals and stuff. We'd gone into serious detail about my Korean diplomat and Shelley's French diplomat—not just their records working for their governments, but their favorite foods, the clothes they wore, what kind of apartments they lived in, and what they liked and didn't like about each other. Shelley's French diplomat had "a strong interest in Korean culture," which was true about Shelley too.

Neither Shelley nor her fake French diplomat had an interest in aliens from the Tau Ceti solar system. Or in best friends who might be mentally ill. Did they?

"Why are you so into Korean stuff?" I said.

Shelley blinked, obviously taken by surprise.

"What?" Shelley didn't actually say, "What does that have to do with anything?" but I could hear it in her voice.

"I mean, why are you so interested in that? What if I decide to drop the Korean thing and switch to something else?"

"Did you get hit on the head or something, Chloe?

We can't start the whole project over! We're already behind now, thanks to you."

"I don't mean the project."

"What does that mean, you don't mean the project?"

"I mean . . ." I sighed. "I don't know what I mean."

Shelley threw her hands into the air.

"Okay, well, let me know when you figure it out."

This time it was Shelley's turn to walk away in a huff. She literally huffed a couple of times, like a buffalo, then stormed off in the direction of the cafeteria. I watched her go, feeling all mixed-up and confused. Then I decided I wasn't hungry, turned around, and headed for the school library instead.

TWENTY

ONE OF THE GOOD THINGS ABOUT GEORGE Matthew K–8 School is the library, and the fact that the school actually lets us go there and use it. It was the best place in school to take a break from people asking me about sushi or talking in nothing but "ching chong" sounds. It was also where I first read *Millicent Min, Girl Genius*, the greatest, funniest book ever written. You're supposed to get an official pass from a teacher and all that stuff, but I was there so much that Ms. Mutch would just wave me in as soon as I appeared in the doorway.

"Hi, Chloe," Ms. Mutch said from the circulation desk, where she was typing furiously away on a computer. She somehow managed to stare at her screen and flash me a wide smile at the same time. "Don't tell me you ate lunch in the hallway again?"

We're not supposed to eat lunch in the hallway, of course, but if you skip the cafeteria and go straight to the library the only other option is to sneak your food into the bathroom and eat it there, and ew, gross. I guess you could also not eat lunch, and there are a ton of girls at school who do, but I don't understand people who don't like food. Today I wasn't hungry at all, though.

"Yeah, I did." I like Ms. Mutch a lot, but if I wasn't telling Shelley the truth, I sure wasn't telling the school librarian, even if she does like fantasy and science fiction.

Oh great. The one adult in town who actually reads books ABOUT aliens from other galaxies, and I couldn't even tell her.

"Where's Shelley?" Ms. Mutch asked, shoveling a little more depression onto my head. Of course Ms. Mutch would ask that; Shelley and I always went to the library together.

"She, uh, had a doctor's appointment," I said.

"Oh, okay." Ms. Mutch did one last hyperactive burst of typing, then dramatically pushed a single key—probably "enter," duh—with her index finger.

"I'm sorry, I was finishing up a post for the school library blog," she said cheerfully. "Now, what can I help you with?"

"I'm fine, I'm . . ." *I'm an alien from another galaxy but it's okay, I come in peace!* "I'm just . . . doing some research, but I don't need any help yet."

It wasn't exactly a lie. I didn't need help with school, I just needed it with life in general.

"Okay, just let me know if you run into any trouble."

I turned away, looking vaguely around the library for a table (they were mostly empty), but then I turned back to Ms. Mutch.

"Actually . . ."

"What do you need, Chloe?" Ms. Mutch was so cheerful, which almost cheered me up too. Almost.

"I need books about aliens."

"Ah, you must be studying immigration in social studies."

"No, not illegal aliens, I mean aliens as in, you know, extraterrestrials."

"Oh." Ms. Mutch blinked rapidly and drummed her fingers on her desktop. "Interesting."

I could tell the question was coming, so I thought fast.

"It's for" — *Think, Cho, think* — "Media Studies, we're doing a project on, uh, urban myths."

"Ah, I see. Well, there are certainly a lot of books to choose from, but I doubt we have very many of them here — you'll probably have better luck at the public library."

Ms. Mutch clattered away at her computer as she

spoke. I heard the low kachunk-thud of something being printed.

"Okay, take a look at these." Ms. Mutch handed me the printout, which had four or five books listed. "That would be a much longer list if I included science-fiction novels, but of course that's not what you need for research purposes."

"Thanks." I took the list and looked at it, then looked back up at Ms. Mutch.

"Ms. Mutch, you like science fiction, right?"

"I sure do. I've been reading it my entire life."

"Can I ask you a question that might sound . . . weird?"

"I specialize in answering weird questions."

"Do you know if there are any science-fiction books where the aliens look like Asian people?"

Ms. Mutch sat up really straight and rubbed her lower lip with her thumb.

"Well, Chloe, that is a VERY interesting question. Very, very interesting. I can't think of any off the top of my head."

She got up and came around to my side of the circulation desk, then stood facing me with her arms crossed and a huge grin on her face.

"Let's take a look, shall we?"

TWENTY-ONE

I SPENT THE ENTIRE LUNCH HOUR LOOKING UP science-fiction books with Ms. Mutch, who I'd always liked but turned out to be some kind of over-the-top genius about science-fiction novels. She'd even written one, which was SO cool.

"I think it's terrific that you're exploring these issues." Ms. Mutch's voice was not-quite-but-almost too loud for the library, although nobody else was in there so it's not like we were bothering the two people who'd just left. "Science fiction and fantasy aren't always used in classrooms, but they can be really useful ways to think about things like racial identity."

She pointed at the cover of the book in my hands.

"Always look at the covers with a critical eye, Chloe. I don't want you to stop reading these books, because it's important to read as wide a variety of books as you can, and a book with a problematic cover can still be enjoyed. But you'll notice—"

She was interrupted by the bell, which took us both by surprise. Ms. Mutch laughed.

"Well, that was a fast lunch hour, wasn't it? I'm sorry I took up so much of your time, but you have some good thoughts about this, Chloe! Thank you so much for talking with me!"

"Thank YOU," I said, really meaning it. I took the books and the even longer list that she'd printed out for me. "I'm gonna check out every one of these."

Which is what I did. I walked to the public library right after school—why the heck not? After talking to Ms. Mutch I knew the children's section wouldn't have too much stuff, so I went straight for the adult science-fiction and fantasy section.

There were tons of alien books there, and I decided to take Ms. Mutch's advice and focus on covers— specifically, I only checked out books that showed human-looking aliens on the covers. I checked out a couple that only had spaceships or whatever on the covers too, just because I thought they looked fun to read, but just a couple.

Mom wasn't teaching that day, so I texted her and asked her to pick me up. When she pulled up in front of the library I staggered to the curb with an armload of books, dropping a few on the sidewalk on the way.

Mom opened the door for me, taking eight or nine books off the top of the stack.

"Not quite as many as usual, huh?" Mom said as we piled books into the trunk of her car. She picked up one of the books, *Tunnel to Oblivion*. "And not for school, I see."

I didn't feel like saying anything to her, so I didn't, and Mom had the brainpower not to push it. We got in the car and drove home in silence. Mom finally spoke again as we pulled into the driveway.

"I hope you won't hate us forever, Chloe," she said in a voice that sounded really, really tired.

"I don't hate you. I just . . ."

I just don't trust you. Which actually felt a hundred times worse, like I was the one stabbing her in the back even though it was the other way around.

"We were trying to protect you. That may not have—"

"Can you open the trunk?" I said, not waiting for an answer as I unbuckled my seat belt, opened the door, and got out to stand by the back of the car. When Mom got out of the car I turned to the side just enough to put her completely out of my field of vision, but I could still hear her sigh right before she popped the trunk open. She silently helped me gather up the books and carry them into the house. When she put her share of the books on the living room table I consolidated them back onto my stack and went straight to my room, not stopping to take off my shoes or anything. I dropped one book, and in the spirit of not stopping I soccer-kicked it along the floor until it slid up against the door to my room.

I went in, shut the door behind me, and didn't come out for three days.

TWENTY-TWO

THE FACT THAT IT WAS THE WEEKEND MADE it easier to stay in my room (mostly) for three days. I spent the whole time reading and analyzing book covers. At some point on Friday night Dad knocked on the door and said something about dinner, but I ignored him, and eventually he went away. I didn't study, or work on the Model UN project, or practice the violin.

I also didn't remember Shelley was supposed to come over on Sunday to work on stuff, but of course she did. I was neck-deep in book analysis by then, and she seemed . . . well, a little freaked out by it.

Mom knocked a bunch of times, but she stopped after Dad talked to her—I couldn't hear what they said, but I heard his voice on the other side of the door right before the knocking stopped. I probably could have found out what he said by rolling my chair over to the door and putting my ear against it, but what was the point? If they were leaving food for me (which they had been) I'd wait until they left to bring it in and eat.

I was halfway through my second book about bug-eyed monsters from space when the knocking started again. "Knocking" wasn't quite accurate, actually: There was only one knock before Shelley opened the door and came in.

She actually kicked the door open—it hit the wall behind it and bounced back hard enough that she had to stop it with her hand. She looked around my room with a slit-eyed look on her face, and I almost felt embarrassed at how messy it was. Almost—it was too dark to actually see the mess. Shelley walked over to the floor lamp and stomped on the on/off button, filling the room with light. I blinked a few times.

"Have you read this?" I waved a handful of potato chips as I held up the book I was reading. "*Interstellar Terror*? The title sucks, but the book's actually pretty good."

"Chloe, what are you doing?"

"I'm reading this book. It's about these aliens who come to Earth, they—"

"Chloe."

"—introduce an alien virus into the water supply, and you know what, the heroes in these movies, the

people who save the world, they're all white people,
ALL OF THEM—"

"Chloe—"

"And when there are human-looking aliens, they're
also all white people! Why don't any of the aliens
who look like white people get killed?"

"Chloe!"

"Where are the Korean people? Why is it always a
white person who saves the world? Why are the aliens
always the bad guys??"

I waved my arms, lost my balance, and almost fell
out of my chair.

"EARTH TO CHLOE!!! WHAT ARE YOU DOING?"

I decided to look at Shelley. "Earth to Chloe. Very
appropriate."

"What do you mean, very appropriate? I've texted
you about a thousand times—know how many times
you've texted back?"

I crammed the handful of potato chips into my
mouth and stared at Shelley, chewing slowly. She made
a circle with her thumb and index finger and stuck it
in my face.

"ZERO," she said. "Some best friend, huh?"

"You're an okay best friend."

"I mean you!" Shelley threw her hands up in the air.

"What are you . . . hey, wait," I said as she grabbed the book out of my hands, looked around for something to use as a bookmark, then defiantly snapped it shut WITHOUT using a bookmark. "I'm reading that. You just lost my place . . ."

"Now you're reading ME. I mean, looking at ME." Shelley spun my chair away from the desk. I grabbed the armrests as she dragged/turned me so I was facing her and pushed me into a corner. The chair thunked against the walls, and I yelped.

"Wow, somebody's had too much sugar today," I said.

"At least I'm not spending all my time sitting in the dark, reading alien invasion books. You look like you've been living in an abandoned school bus!"

"Hey, there's totally a book where the aliens do that! *Bus Driver from the Stars*—it's for little kids so it's kind of stupid—"

Shelley smacked a palm against her face and abruptly sat on the bed. She bounced a couple of times, palm still pressed against her face, then dropped both hands into her lap and glared at me with her head tilted forward. I looked down at my lap, which was covered with potato chips. I picked one up and held it out.

"Want a potato chip?"

"No, I want you to snap out of it. You know we have a bajillion Model UN assignments to work on, right?"

I shrugged.

"Have you been working on them?"

"What are you, my mother?"

"I'm your FRIEND, Chloe. I know, you don't care anymore, and I don't know why I still do, but I do. I guess I'm also an idiot."

"You're not an idiot," I said in a quiet voice, looking down at my hands.

"No I'm not, but you sure are acting like one."

I felt a sizzle of anger when she said that.

"You don't have any idea what's going on with me, Shelley."

"No DUH, Chloe, you haven't actually TOLD me what's going on with you! If you tell me what's going on with you then I'LL KNOW WHAT'S GOING ON WITH YOU!"

The anger went away, poof, and I stared at Shelley helplessly.

"I can't tell you. You wouldn't . . ."

Believe me.

". . . understand."

"Yes I would."

I sighed and put my hands over my face.

"No you wouldn't. You'd think I'm crazy. When my parents told me, I thought THEY were crazy."

"I won't think you're crazy."

"Well, you'll think I'm weird, then. Very, very weird."

"Guess what, Cho, I already think you're weird. You know why?"

"N—" I guess it was a rhetorical question, because Shelley kept right on going.

"Because when you get hurt playing soccer you refuse to come out of the game; because I actually think you can play the sadistic violin solo that Adam can't even begin to play; because I'm pretty sure you'd be willing to get in a fistfight with anyone who's being a bully; because you've already kissed a boy—"

"Yecch, I haven't kissed any boys!" I sat up quickly enough to make the swivel chair roll backward, which made me lose my balance and spill potato chip crumbs all over the rug.

"You're such a liar, but whatever. My point is, you're extremely weird."

"Gee whiz, thanks."

"Chloe, you hang out with me, the biggest weirdo in the entire school. The only thing I'm good at is grades. You're good at everything, including being a best friend. At least you used to be good at that."

Shelley crossed her arms and stared at the wall behind me, and I realized she wasn't just mad — she was also about to cry.

Aaaack! I was the worst best friend ever.

"I'm sorry," I said.

Silence.

"I'm a total jerk."

"Yes you are," Shelley said. "NOW go back to the 'I'm sorry' part."

"I'm sorry."

Shelley leaned over with her elbows on her knees, still cross-legged on the bed.

"SO WHAT'S GOING ON?"

I took a deep breath and blew it out noisily.

"You really will think I'm crazy."

"WHAT'S GOING ON, CHLOE?"

"My parents finally decided to talk to me about being Korean, and they said we're actually" — another deep breath — "aliens."

Shelley blinked.

"Meaning what, you're illegal aliens? Like you could be deported?"

"No, not that. We're aliens. From outer space."

Silence.

"Not Korean, in other words."

I tried to make it sound all casual and jokey, but

my throat was like a tunnel coated with sandpaper, and it came out kind of raspy instead.

Shelley's eyebrows were a crinkly disaster area. She opened her mouth, closed it, opened it again, started laughing, then slowly and gradually stopped laughing when I just kept staring at her. I don't know if it showed on my face, but that was when I realized how desperate I was. I really, really needed Shelley to believe me.

"Wow, you're serious," she said.

"Have I ever lied to you? About anything?" I pushed my hair back from my face and squeezed the top of my head with both hands.

"You mean recently? Like when you didn't come to my house before school that one day?"

"Oh, right. I'd just found out the night before . . ."

"No kidding. Do you really think I can't tell when you're lying?"

"Well, no, I mean . . . I just . . ."

"Yeah, I know what you mean. Until THAT TIME, no, I guess not. But Chloe, this is . . . you know?"

"I know."

"Do you have . . ." Shelley waved her hands in circles on either side of her head. ". . . proof?"

"Yeah."

As we went out to the greenhouse I told her the details of the conversation with my parents, my conversation with Ms. Lee, and all of the strange websites for people who think they're aliens to talk to each other.

"The people on sites like *Abduction Reconstruction* are really OUT THERE, though," I said as I opened the greenhouse door. I caught the look on Shelley's face and sighed. "I know, I know—I sound out there too. I *know*."

"I didn't say anything," Shelley said as she closed the door behind her.

We went to the big plastic tub of plants and fish in the middle of the greenhouse, the one with Dad's special variety of "koi."

"This is gonna be gross," I said, more to myself than to Shelley. I dunked a hand into the tub as Shelley watched with a worried look on her face. I wondered if I'd even be able to catch one, and if I couldn't, how I'd convince Shelley I wasn't crazy, when a fish practically swam right into my hand.

"Huh," I said, lifting the fish out of the water.

"Wow, did you just catch that with your bare hand?" Shelley said, impressed.

"Uh, sort of. Okay . . ."

I held the fish up at chin level, trying to decide where to lick it. The fish wasn't wiggling or anything, which was bizarre enough, but it also seemed like it was looking at me, which was off-the-charts bizarre. Except it wasn't, now that Mom and Dad had whipped out a whole new set of charts.

I dabbed at the fish's side with my tongue, trying to block out the "AAUGH!" sound Shelley made. I had my eyes mostly shut, but I didn't close them all the way because I didn't want to lick the fish's eyeballs by mistake, so I saw the spot where my tongue landed immediately start glowing. I almost spit right on the floor of the greenhouse, but then I remembered how Dad did it. I spit into the tub, then dropped the fish back in.

"That is so gross," Shelley said, but she also walked up to me.

"Is that enough proof for you?" I said. I turned around and spit into the tub again.

"Yeah, I guess. There isn't any way a normal human being can glow like that."

"Normal." I laughed, then turned and spit again, even though nothing was coming out of my mouth. "You should just say 'human being'—not even an abnormal human could do that."

"So . . . this is why you've been so whatever lately, huh? Hey, are you okay?"

Shelley put a hand on my shoulder, I guess to keep me steady, but I suddenly couldn't see straight.

"Yeah, I'm okay . . . well, maybe I'm not . . . I feel . . ."

"Chloe? Chlooooeeeeee?" Shelley's voice got all drawn out like it was being played at half-speed, and her face turned into kind of a starburst of blurriness, and then I don't know what happened because everything went kerblooey and I passed out.

TWENTY-THREE

My memories of first grade are pretty fuzzy, with a few exceptions. There was that time our teacher Mrs. King got a new book for the classroom that I couldn't wait for her to read. But then she read it while I was out sick, and wouldn't read it again the next day. There was the day Marie Philips, who was almost a third best friend with me and Shelley, moved away. The thing I remember best, though, was the time when Mom picked me up from school and Mrs. King pulled her aside to talk.

"You must be so proud of Chloe," Mrs. King said as kids and parents milled around inside and in front of the classroom. "She's such a gifted child."

"Thank you, we are," Mom said, looking down at me with a smile and stroking my hair over and over. "She makes us proud every day."

I smiled back, ridiculously happy, ignoring the other kids who were giving me mean looks as if it were my fault their parents weren't saying stuff like that to them.

"It must be so stimulating for Chloe to have two scientists for parents!"

"We try to keep things interesting for her. Don't we, big girl?"

"Yeah," I said, leaning backward against Mom and turning my face up to look at her. In first grade my head only came up to Mom's waist, and when I looked up like that her face was like something floating in the sky.

That dreamy first-grade moment seemed far, far in the past when I opened my eyes to the sight of Mom leaning over me with a plastic cup in her hand. The cup said FENTON'S CREAMERY on it, with a picture of a rocket ship surrounded by stars and swirly planets. Of course.

"You just had to try it for yourself, huh, big girl?" Mom said with a one-sided smile. I guess she wasn't mad—she never calls me "big girl" when she's mad. She actually hadn't called me "big girl" in a long, long time, and it might have made me get choked up if I didn't already feel like I was about to puke.

Waking up on the floor of your dad's aquaponic greenhouse isn't very pleasant. That floor's always at least a little bit wet, first of all, and it's a green, fishy, smelly kind of wetness. I could feel it in the hair on the back of my head. I could feel it on my scalp.

"Mrrggle," I said, or something like that.

"We expected you to tell Shelley, but not in such a dramatic way," Mom said.

"Proof," I said. "Needed proof . . ."

Shelley was silent, which was probably the smart choice.

"Here, swish this around in your mouth," Mom said as I sat up with a groan.

"My head hurts," I mumbled.

"The fish enzymes don't affect us all the same way," Mom said. "You don't have a lot of tolerance built up, you know. Swish."

She raised the cup to my lips, and I backed away at its stink.

"Gah, vinegar? Ech."

"You don't have to DRINK it, just swishing it in your mouth is enough. It's only a tablespoon or so, and it'll make your head feel better."

I wanted my head to feel better more than I wanted to say no to Mom, so I held my breath, poured the vinegar into my mouth, and swished it around. My tongue and gums tingled briefly, and what do you know, I felt better almost right away. I got up on my knees and spit the vinegar into the plant/fish tub.

"This greenhouse is a lot less appealing than it used to be," Shelley said.

"Do I have to worry about growing a third eyeball or something?" I asked Mom without really looking at her.

"No third eyeballs, you'll be fine."

"Is there anything cool about being from Tau Ceti?" I said in a sour voice as I stood up. "Mind control? Teleportation? A hyperdrive spaceship buried under the house? Or is making a fish glow by licking it the only thing?"

Mom sighed. It was strange to hear Mom sigh so often.

"One of the reasons we came here is because we really are almost an exact match, genetically speaking. You should be able to have babies with someone who was born on Earth."

"BLECH," Shelley and I said at the same time. Thinking about having babies did not make my head feel better.

"Let's get you inside." Mom and Shelley helped me stand up and walked me into the house. I'll give Mom some credit—she let me and Shelly go into my room without saying a word, and she left us alone once we were in there.

"Do you need to lie down or anything?" Shelley asked. I shook my head no, and she sat on the bed while I poked at the stack of science-fiction books on the desk.

"So . . ." Shelley said. "This is different."

"At least you're still a normal human."

"I don't know about *normal*. Or even human — aren't we 99.999 percent genetically the same, or something like that? How is that not human?"

"It's 0.001 percent not human, is how. Oh, I haven't even showed you this—" I looked around, picked a crumpled sheet of paper off of the floor, and handed it to Shelley. "The GeneGenie test result. You know what it says?"

Shelley took the paper and quickly scanned it.

"Read the paragraph right under 'Dear Ms. Cho.'"

"*There are zero matches for your profile in the GeneGenie ancestry database, possibly because of sample contamination. Please submit a new sample and we'll retest at no additional charge.* Huh."

"See?" I held up my hands, palms to the sky in a what-are-you-gonna-do gesture. "Zero matches. Zero percent human."

"But so what? You grew up here; you've spent your

entire life eating the same terrible food at the Hedge Diner as I have; how are you not human? And what's with all the sci-fi books?"

"Duh, aliens."

"Uh, okay. Are you . . . doing research?"

"Cultural research! Have you ever looked at book covers? I mean, REALLY looked at them?"

Shelley nodded, slowly and unconvincingly. I started grabbing books and waving them in the air.

"Look at this one, *Moonrise on Gamma 14*—white aliens! Or this, *Perihelion*—white aliens again! Or this piece of garbage, *Schrödinger's Schnauzer*—more white aliens, plus it's a terrible book!"

I flung each book down on the bed in front of Shelley, who was looking at me while sitting very still.

"Oh, this one has BLUE aliens, sure, I guess that's their excuse for giving them blue eyes that are big and round—they're blue aliens, but they're really white aliens, right?"

I slammed *My Blue Heaven* down on the bed with both hands, crossed my arms, and looked at Shelley.

"Right?"

Shelley stared for a second, like she was trying to figure out what to say.

"I guess. Can I ask you a question?"

"What?"

"Do you think you should . . . I don't know . . . maybe see a doctor or something?"

Well, that was unexpected.

"Why? I'm not sick."

"I mean like a psychiatrist."

"Oh my god, you didn't just . . ." Grrrr. "I'm not mentally ill, Shelley. Do you not believe the alien thing anymore?"

"I totally believe you, that's actually why I wonder if you should see a psychiatrist or something. Finding out you're from outer space seems . . . stressful."

"Duh, of course it's stressful."

"You remember how intense Dana Smithfield was all the way up till third grade, until her mom took her to that doctor in the city and she got so much calmer?"

"Dana has ADHD; she's less intense because she takes meds. I don't think they have any 'stop being an alien' meds."

"I'm just saying, it might be more useful than getting all worked up over book covers."

"IT'S NOT JUST THE COVERS."

"I know, I know."

"And what's with the psychiatrist thing?"

"Well, my mom IS one, you know."

"So what? That makes you an expert now? You're going around telling everybody to make appointments with your mom now?"

"No." Shelley frowned. "But this isn't, you know, normal."

Et tu, Shelley? "What do you mean, not normal??"

"I don't mean . . ." Shelley sighed. "Come on, you have to admit—"

"Admit what? That I'm abnormal?"

"You're an alien, Chloe. I don't know any other aliens."

"I guess it was more normal when you thought I was just Korean, huh?" I lurched up and off of the bed hard enough to send papers flying and make Shelley topple over on her side.

"Hey! What's that supposed to mean?" Shelley gave me a hard-core furrowed-brow stare as she pushed herself back up into a sitting position.

"Nothing, it's just you're so into my being Korean, but now that I'm from outer space you're all 'OMG MENTAL ILLNESS' and stuff . . ."

"What are you talking about?? I'm not 'so into' your being Korean!"

"You so are. You *said* how cool being Korean would be, remember?"

You could have shoved a tennis ball into Shelley's

mouth without touching anything, lips, teeth, whatever.

"That was second grade! Have you been holding a grudge this whole time?"

"SO YOU REMEMBER!" I shouted, pointing in triumph. Victory!

Shelley dragged her hands down the length of her face, making her eyes, nose, and mouth go all rubbery for a second.

"You know what, I'm really not in the mood to be yelled at."

"I'M NOT YELLING."

"Remember when we used to do fun things like talk about books and not yell at each other like howler monkeys?" Shelley said with a scowl. "I miss those days."

"Fine, abandon me now that I'm not Korean enough. Whatever."

"God, Chloe, what's wrong with you??" Shelley barked. "Why are you being so weird?"

"Oh sure, now I'm weird. LOOK AT THE ALIEN GIRL, SHE'S EVEN WEIRDER THAN WHEN SHE WAS KOREAN."

"You're just proving my point," Shelley said.

"You wouldn't understand," I said.

"You know what, you're right. I don't understand.

I just wanted to hang out, but you're too busy yelling about book covers and acting completely bizarre. Whatever."

Shelley grabbed her backpack and slung it over her shoulder with a hard, fast twist of her arm. The backpack hit her back hard enough to bounce, but she didn't seem to notice.

"Call me when you're interested in not being an idiot, okay?" Shelley said in a superhigh, fake-polite voice.

"Why don't YOU?" I said.

"In your dreams."

"Fine, see if I care."

"I can see right now. You don't."

Shelley stomped across the house and out the front door, slamming it behind her.

"Whatever," I muttered. I looked down at the books still scattered on the bed. Paleface aliens as far as the eye could see. Being Korean had never gotten in the way of being friends with Shelley, but now that we both knew what I really was it was like *I am Chloe Cho and I do not come in peace.* I guess I'd pushed her too far, like using a reverse tractor beam, ha-ha.

I shoved the books off of the bed and flopped down face first.

I stayed there for a long time.

TWENTY-FOUR

SCHOOL IS A TOTALLY DIFFERENT EXPERIENCE WHEN you do everything alone. You talk a lot less, and it takes less time to get from place to place. It's also more lonely, but hey, what's lonelier than being an alien from another world?

At least I could talk about being Korean without making people think I'm insane, and Korean people are 100 percent human, not 99.999 percent human like me. I wanted to be all human again. I spent the whole day floating around, thinking about science-fiction book covers, lying rat-fink parents, and DNA tests. Then it was time for orchestra.

Shelley and I avoided each other on the way into orchestra, which we'd been doing in every other class we had together so hey, nothing new there. I sat down, opened my case, and stared at my violin. It was so pretty, and it sounded so good, and Mom only bought it in a desperate try to avoid telling me anything about being Korean! Gah! I poked at the strings, feeling depressed.

"Okay, everybody, let's start with a few scales."

I looked up at the sound of Mrs. DeRosa's voice. Mrs. DeRosa? Why was she conducting today?

"Chloe Cho!"

And why was Mr. C calling me from the door to the office, holding a notepad and a stack of papers, doing a lame punching-the-air thing that was kind of funny even though it was lame?

Oh.

First-chair competition. Crap.

"Bring that shiny new ax on in here," Mr. C said cheerfully.

I stared down at my "ax," trying to remember what piece I was supposed to have practiced for the competition. I looked quickly at Adam, who was visibly gulping as he ran a finger over the sheet music on his music stand.

"Uh . . ." I cleverly said.

"Come on, no time like the present," Mr. C said.

I got up reeeeally slowly and walked past Mr. C and into the office as the rest of the orchestra started warming up behind me.

The music office is between the orchestra room and

the choir room, and since the choir room doesn't have a class in it at the same time as orchestra, we always do first-chair challenges in there.

"Got your music?" Mr. C said as he walked across the office and opened the choir room door. The choir room is almost identical to the orchestra room, except it isn't filled with instrument cases and music stands. There was just one stand in there, in front of a pair of empty chairs.

Did I have my music? "I think I left it at home," I said, which was only a partial lie. I had no idea at all where it was, so it could have been at home, but I'd definitely left it somewhere.

Mr. C clucked his tongue, but he was obviously in a good mood.

"Lucky for you I have a copy of everything," he said, shuffling through his fistful of paper and fishing out a few sheets that he plopped down on the music stand.

I stood there, suddenly overwhelmed by the strange feeling of not being ready to play—I hadn't practiced the music at all.

"Mr. C . . ."

"Yes?" Mr. C said as he adjusted the chairs so he was facing my chair at a right angle from the music stand, so he could see me but I couldn't see him.

"..."

Mr. C sat down and grinned.

"Not nervous, are you?"

No, just not ready, I thought. I'd been about to ask if I could reschedule my time, but then I thought, *Why? Who cares?*

So instead I sat down, took out my violin, and sight-read the piece that I hadn't practiced at all.

TWENTY-FIVE

In sixth grade I dominated the fall orchestra concert, and I mean total domination—I owned that concert. When it was time for the orchestra to set up I walked out of the orchestra room and onto the stage in my usual state of terror, wishing I'd practiced just fifteen minutes more per day, wanting to make Mom and Dad think *That's our daughter and she is AWESOME* without knowing if I actually would, and so on. I fanned out my sheet music on the music stand without letting my hands shake, but just barely.

The real concert, at night, with a real audience, was so much better than playing the school assembly the day before, which was always full of troublemakers making noise and throwing spitballs and stuff. It was also so much worse, because everyone was actually paying attention. When the curtain went up and everyone clapped for us it was exciting and terrifying at the same time.

"Okay, people, let's dazzle 'em," Mr. C said, and we

did. The fourth-grade fall concert was fun just because it was my first, and the holiday concerts were always fun, even if the actual holiday music wasn't that hard, but that first sixth-grade concert was the best because EVERYONE played really well. Adam was second chair, of course, and even he sounded good, fancypants violin, perfectly ironed clothes, and all.

When it was time for my solo I took a deep breath, flexed my bow arm once, and dove in, and I realized I was FEELING IT, even though it was in the middle of the hardest piece we'd ever played since I'd started orchestra, and it was also the hardest solo I'd ever played. The sixty hours I'd spent practicing just that solo during the month before the concert really paid off. I was in such a zone that I probably could have played it with my eyes closed. I didn't miss a single note, even during the thirty-second-note runs; my portamentos were perfectly arched rainbows of sound; and I played the dynamic notations like a boss.

There was a huge burst of applause when I finished the solo, and when the entire string section made a wall of sound on the final crescendo it felt like my heart would burst right out of my chest, like the Incredible Hulk bursting out of his shirt. On the final note Mr. C held both arms way up over his head, his baton in one hand, and when he snapped his arms down we slammed the door on that song as well as it could be done.

We always get standing ovations—I think it's probably illegal for parents not to give their kids in orchestra a standing ovation—but that one was different. Shelley's mom and dad practically jumped out of their seats. Mom and Dad were in the third row, and other parents were actually turning around to congratulate them.

Adam bumped me with his elbow. He was grinning so hard it looked like the top of his head would fall off.

"You were AWESOME, Chloe!" he said, and he was so goofily cheerful that I couldn't help but like him.

"Thanks, Adam!"

"Abigail Yang better watch out, you're breathing down her neck!"

OH COME ON. Of all the times to pull out the old Abigail Yang thing . . . I wasn't surprised, but geez.

Still, even Adam in Clueless Mode couldn't ruin it when Mr. C caught my eye, gave me a big thumbs-up, turned to the crowd, and gestured for me to stand. That was a first, not just for me, but for anyone during my three years in orchestra. It was the best moment of my entire orchestra career. It was one of the best moments of my whole life.

So you know, I'm used to Mr. C talking to me in a certain way—he jokes around a lot, he keeps talking about Abigail Freaking Yang, but it's always clear he expects me to be awesome, and I always HAD been awesome, so no problems, right? This time was different, though. He looked . . . droopy? Like all of his facial hair was hanging straight down.

Oh, right. He looked disappointed.

"Chloe, I'll be honest, I didn't expect to have this conversation with you unless some hotshot new kid joined the orchestra," Mr. C said, looking sadly at me from behind his desk. "You've always been so far ahead of the pack."

I lost, I thought.

Did I care?

"Adam Wheeler won first chair," he said, sounding more businesslike. "I know he worked really hard for it"—emphasis on *worked really hard*, and oh look, another first; no teacher had dropped hints about working hard to me before—"and you'll get the chance to win it back next year, of course."

"Okay," I said. Mr. C's eyebrows went up.

"Is something going on?" he said. "You haven't been yourself lately."

"Fine."

"If there's anything—"

"I'm fine."

Mr. C blew out a breath, which made his mustache flutter for a second, and shook his head.

"Okay, well, I hope that's true. Second chair is just as important as first chair, you know, and I——" Pause. "——trust you to do a great job at it."

I cared, but I also didn't care, you know what I mean? At least I thought I didn't care, but then I walked out of Mr. C's office into the orchestra room, saw everyone milling around, saw Adam sitting in the first-chair seat, and realized I couldn't tell him to get his sorry butt out of it.

Oh right, I did care, and it was too late. I was second chair. I was a LOSER.

Adam and Phil Leder were talking with big smiles on their faces, but when Phil saw me coming he stopped smiling. He gave Adam a quick high five, nodded in my direction, and made a fast getaway. Adam didn't stop smiling when he saw me but he did tone it down a little. In fact, he looked . . . what was that look? Nervous?

Sympathetic? *Sorry?* Oh great. That made it impossible to hate him.

"Hey, Chloe," he said. "So . . ."

"Congratulations," I said, feeling like a zombie and probably sounding like one.

"Are you okay, Chloe?"

Oh man, Adam was being NICE. *Stop, Adam, stop . . .*

"What, did you think I was gonna cry about it or something?" I sat down in the Loser Chair, the second-seat chair, which was right next to Adam; gee, it just kept getting better and better. "You're first chair, congrats, whatever."

"I just, you know," Adam said. "I was just wondering."

"You don't look all broken up about it," I grumbled.

"I just know you're better than how you played in the competition, you know?"

"How do you know? Because I'm Korean? Because you think I've been playing the violin since I was two years old or something?"

Adam blinked.

"No, because you're always been the best violin player in school. What is going on with you?"

"What's going on is I found out my parents are aliens from another galaxy, which technically makes ME an alien from another galaxy!" It felt like my eyeballs were giving off sparks. "Does that explain it? Are you satisfied?"

Adam leaned away from me and held up his hands, frowning.

"Whatever, Chloe. You don't have to be so sarcastic."

He put his violin under his chin and started tuning up. I took my violin out of its case, but instead of tuning it I just looked at it. I was still staring at it when Mr. C came out of the music office with his baton in hand. He gave me a small, semi-cheerful smile that I probably would have appreciated if looking at him didn't make me feel totally humiliated.

"All right now, big day today, let's congratulate all our first chairs—on bassoon, Kelly Vernick! Take a bow, Kelly!"

The room burst into applause. Kelly, red-haired and gangly, stood up with a huge grin on her face and quickly bobbed her head in all directions, including behind her where there was nothing but a wall. A bunch of people laughed.

"First-chair cello, Ben Feinberg! Take a bow, Ben!"

Ben was our ONLY cello player so it wasn't like he had to slay a dragon or something, but everyone clapped for him anyway. He did a presidential wave with one hand.

"First-chair viola, Shelley Drake!"

WHAT??

There were a few gasps of surprise, then a round of applause as Shelley stood up, but I could only stare at her with my mouth hanging open. Shelley did that half-smile thing that always makes people think she's stuck-up even though it really means she's nervous, but she was looking at me with a worried crinkle in her eyebrows.

I couldn't take it. Shelley was first chair, and I wasn't — the natural order of the universe was completely off! I looked away, but not before seeing the hurt look come across her face.

What did she care?? It sucked, yeah, and I suddenly felt awful and sad, but it wasn't like we were still best friends or anything. Anyway, I knew the big moment of retch was about to arrive, and sure enough . . .

"First-chair violin, Adam Wheeler!"

This time it wasn't just a handful of gasps — the entire room sucked in a giant lungful of air and let it out, WUH-HUH, at the same time. Lifelong third chair violin Samantha Castle said "OH. MY. GOD," not even trying to whisper, and then the entire backstabbing orchestra started clapping. Not just clapping, really, it was almost like people were trying to hurt their hands by banging them against each other. I don't know which was worse, losing first chair or seeing how happy the entire orchestra was about Adam winning it.

Adam stood up, grinning from ear to ear. I thought

he was deliberately not looking at me, which probably would have been a smart move since I kind of
wanted to pull his heart right out of his chest and
make him look at it, but he glanced at me out of the
corner of one eye. His grin flickered, and instead of
wallowing in the applause any longer he sat down.

"Yes, yes, congratulations, everyone — this is the
first time in four years we have new first chairs for
every section, so well done, you guys. And for those
of you who did your best but didn't get where you
want to be, I'm still proud of you for making the effort.
Even Abigail Yang lost a few competitions on her way
to the top!"

Something went KABLOOEY inside my brain.

"What's that supposed to mean?" I said, and it
came out REALLY loud, because the room went completely, pin-drop, algebra-test silent. I suddenly had
Mr. C's undivided attention.

"Excuse me, Chloe?" he said, in a voice that was a
little too calm.

"Do you not know I'm not Abigail Flipping Yang,
or can you really just not tell us apart? That would be
stupid, since I'm actually *here*."

"Chloe. You need to dial it back *right now.*" Mr. C's
hands were on his hips, and he leaned forward in a way
that I knew meant business, but I just didn't CARE.

"What if I wasn't even Korean? Would you still bring her up all the time, or would you have to find some other violin player to talk about?"

"Chloe. Mr. Frank's office, right now."

Mr. C doesn't get really mad too often, but when he does he knows how to yell without yelling, if you know what I mean. When he uses *that voice* it pretty much goes right through your flesh and into your skeleton. I stared at him for a second, then packed up my violin, got out of my chair with a clatter, and stomped away. I ignored Shelley as I passed the viola players, left the orchestra room, and headed to the vice principal's office for the first time in my entire life.

TWENTY-SIX

Mrs. McBeal, the school's office manager, looked up from her desk as I walked into the school office. She was talking to Ms. Wilson, and they both looked surprised when I trudged up to the counter without saying hello or anything.

"I need to talk to Mr. Frank."

"Whatever for, Chloe?" Ms. Wilson was actually one of the youngest teachers in the school—Ms. Lee might have been the only one who was younger—but for some reason she always said stuff like "whatever for" and "oh my stars," which made her sound a thousand years old. I was even more annoyed by it than usual.

"Mr. Coppinger sent me," I mumbled. Wow, that was humiliating to say. Being sent to the office was so humiliating! Which I guess was the whole point.

"Beg pardon?" Aaack, *beg pardon*? Who says that?

"MR. COPPINGER SENT ME TO TALK TO MR. FRANK," I said, not quite shouting.

"Well now, that is a surprise," Mrs. McBeal said with a frown. "Chloe Cho being sent to Mr. Frank? There must be some mistake."

I looked at her, and my face suddenly felt like somebody had cranked its temperature up by fifty degrees. I liked Mrs. McBeal. She was always nice to everyone, even kids who were in trouble. I knew she wasn't being sarcastic, and I had to stop looking at her and look at the countertop instead, because there wasn't any mistake. I pointed vaguely toward Mr. Frank's door.

"I'm sorry, Mrs. McB," I said in a much lower voice. "Is he in there?"

"Yes, he is," Mrs. McBeal said. "You've really been sent to see him?"

I nodded, still looking down. I heard a click and a burst of fuzzy noise.

"Mr. Frank, Chloe Cho is here from Mr. Coppinger's class," Mrs. McBeal said.

The intercom is probably a thousand years old — it'd probably work equally well to just holler — but I was still able to hear Mr. Frank's response.

"*Who's* here?"

"Chloe Cho." Mrs. McBeal might have been saying "two thirty" to someone who'd just asked what time it is, and I appreciated it. All the what-do-you-mean-it's-Chloe-Cho stuff wasn't making me feel any better.

"Okay, send her in."

Mrs. McBeal nodded at me, a single, crisp down-and-up motion. Ms. Wilson, on the other hand, got this *look* on her face, like she was really sad or something. I thought how punching a teacher was probably an especially bad idea when I was already in trouble, so I just opened Mr. Frank's office door and went in.

Mr. Frank looked up from his desk and put down his pen as I came into his office. The windows behind him looked out on the parking lot, so it was a little bit hard to look at him with glare from the sun bouncing off the windshields of the cars and into my eyes.

"Chloe Cho." Everyone in school says Mr. Frank is like a robot — when he talks you can't tell what he's thinking or feeling. Not at all. Ever. Not even if he's expelling you from school, although obviously I'd never seen that happen.

"This is quite a surprise," he said, leaning back in his chair. He put his fingertips together in an upside-down V and tapped them against his mouth a couple of times. "You're absolutely the last person I'd expect to see in here. Do you want to tell me what happened?"

No, I thought, but I told him anyway. He sat there without moving and stared at me from behind his big square glasses, his light brown hair in kind of a helmet shape. I was really irritated by the stripes on his tie because they looked like candy canes. I hate candy canes.

". . . and he told me to come here."

Mr. Frank tapped his V-shaped fingercluster against his lips a couple times more, then leaned back in his chair.

"I'm really surprised by this, Miss Cho, and I'm not easy to surprise," he said. "I imagine your parents wouldn't be very pleased if I were to call them."

"You're gonna call my parents?" Gah, I didn't know he did that. There was a whole hidden world of stuff that happens when you get sent to the vice principal's office. "Do you, um, have to?"

"No, but I'm considering it. Insubordinate behavior in the classroom is no joke, Miss Cho."

I know, I almost said. I really did know, and I had to look down at the floor again. You know what's not fun, especially when you can't help yourself from doing it? Looking at the floor because you're too embarrassed to look up.

"Especially from a student like you, who's always been so compliant."

Compliant? What did that mean? Obedient? Like a dog?

"I'm rather interested in talking to your parents, actually. I'd like to better understand their perspective on your education."

Okay, that got me to look up.

"What do you mean, their . . . perspective?"

Mr. Frank raised one eyebrow. Maybe he wasn't used to kids saying anything in these meetings.

"Meaning, I think there's always something to be learned from cultures different from ours," he said. "I can't imagine this is what your parents expect from you."

What did *that* mean? And how did Mr. Frank have any business talking about what my parents expect?

"Why not?" I said, feeling my face get hot and not caring that Mr. Frank was the vice principal. "How do you know what my parents expect? How long have you been able to read minds?"

"Excuse me?" Mr. Frank put his hands on the desk and sat up really straight. I'd finally gotten him to do something other than lean back in his chair with his hands folded like an evil mad scientist, which was probably not a smart thing to do, but screw it.

"And what are you talking about, *cultures different from ours*? What are you trying to say? Are you some kind of racist?"

"Miss Cho."

"This stupid town is full of racists, I don't know why you'd be any different—"

"MISS CHO."

Mr. Frank was halfway out of his seat, with a severe frown on his face. A thought went flying through my brain—*Oh, he looks like a real person when he's mad!*—and I almost said it out loud.

"I am very, very tempted to issue you detention, Miss Cho. This is unacceptable behavior. Absolutely unacceptable."

I glared at him, not feeling apologetic at all, but I didn't say anything else.

Mr. Frank stared me down (he tried to, anyway), then slowly sat in his chair again.

"I'm a fair man, Miss Cho," he said. "I could punish you right now—I probably *should* punish you right now—but I believe in taking a student's permanent record into account, and yours has always been exemplary."

Whatever, I thought, but I guess my sense of self-preservation had kicked back in—I kept my mouth shut.

"Now if you're ready to hear it, I'll answer your question: You're not the only Asian person I've ever met, Miss Cho. Koreans have many praiseworthy qualities—"

???!!!

" —not the least of which is a commitment to education that many of our own parents frankly do not have, so—"

OUR OWN PARENTS? My parents didn't qualify as "our own," huh?

" —after all of the sacrifices your parents must have made to come here—"

"Oh, you have no idea," I blurted out. "Just shut up."

"EXCUSE me??" Mr. Frank actually got up out of his chair.

"I SAID, shut up, you don't know what—"

"ENOUGH, MISS CHO."

"It's not enough, you're an *idiot*—"

"THAT. IS. ENOUGH!"

We locked eyes, student and principal, mano a mano.

"One week of detention," Mr. Frank said, staring me in the eye.

Fine, I thought.

TWENTY-SEVEN

DETENTION, WHICH TURNED OUT TO BE NOT ALL that fine, was held in room 134 with Mr. Dombrowski, English teacher and my personal nemesis. The second I walked into the room I could tell the difference between detention and normal class. People weren't even pretending to study or anything — everyone was talking, sitting on desks, throwing stuff, and totally ignoring Mr. Dombrowski, who sat behind the desk at the front of the room, reading a magazine. Worst teacher ever.

Of course right after I walked into the room it went dead silent and everybody turned and stared at me. It wasn't friendly staring — some of the stares looked mean, some of them looked confused, and they all looked surprised. None of them looked friendly, though.

Like I cared. I stared back, only stopping when Mr. Dombrowski woke up from his coma and actually said my name.

"Ah, Chloe Cho. You're new to these parts, aren't you?"

"I guess so," I said, cool as an ice cube. No way was I letting Dumb-Dumbrowski get under my skin.

"Well, find yourself a seat, and good luck."

I spotted an empty seat up front—of course, none of these people would ever choose to sit up front if they could avoid it—so I trudged over and more or less fell into it, dropping my backpack on the floor next to me. The boy in the seat next to me leaned in my direction. I didn't lean away from him, but I didn't bother reacting to him until he spoke.

"What'd you do?" he said. I finally turned to look at him.

"None of your business," I said.

"You're just, you know, Chloe Straight-A+ Student Cho, but *you have detention*! What'd you do?"

"I talked back to a teacher, okay? Are you happy?"

"Oh," he said, looking disappointed. "That's it, huh? That's kind of boring."

". . . with Shelley Drake, but not anymore . . ."

What?? Somebody in the back of the room was talking about me and Shelley.

"You should totally start a trash-can fire or something, just to REALLY blow your reputation," said Annoying Kid.

"Shut up!" I said, trying to hear the conversation behind me.

It was no good, though — whoever'd been talking about me and Shelley was talking about something else. Either that or I just couldn't hear them anymore.

I never knew before how boring detention is. You're allowed to do homework, but I didn't feel like doing homework, and I didn't have a book to read, so there was nothing else to do except pick spitballs out of my hair, which I had to do twice. I felt the first one hit my head, but just barely, and the burst of idiotic giggling from the back of the room was a pretty obvious clue about who'd done it. I picked the disgusting little glob of wet paper out of my hair, dropped it on the floor, and glared at the back of the room as I wiped my hand on my leg.

"Face front, Miss Cho," Mr. Dombrowski said, and I spun around to look at him with my mouth open in shock.

"Why are you calling ME out?? They're the ones throwing spitballs!" I pointed furiously over my shoulder with one thumb.

"Nobody gets special treatment in here, Miss Cho, not even you," Mr. Dombrowski said, leaning back in his chair.

"But I didn't DO any—"

"Miss Cho, I know you think highly of yourself, and I know you don't have problems questioning authority, and that's all well and good, but I'm hearing some uncharacteristic things about your recent behavior. There are no pedestals in this room, Miss Cho, not even for you."

I sat very, very still. No teacher had ever spoken to me like that before. Ever.

"Do your time like everyone else, Miss Cho. Keep your mouth closed, do your time, and it'll be over soon enough."

There was a very, very low giggle from the back of the room, but Mr. Dombrowski pretended not to hear it, and I sank into my chair in defeat.

It's going to be a long week, I thought.

TWENTY-EIGHT

THREE MORNINGS LATER WHEN MY ALARM CLOCK went off I whacked it randomly a few times until it stopped, lay there for five minutes until it went off again, hit it again, lay there for five minutes until it went off again, then put the pillow on top of my head when Dad knocked on the door.

"Go away," I said from under the pillow.

"Excuse me?" Dad's voice said from the other side of the door. "Honey, it's time to get up. Also, your alarm clock is making me feel a little agitated."

"I'm up, I'm up." I sank a little deeper into the bed.

"Can I come in?"

"Mmmmffrrgghh," I said, facedown on the mattress.

I heard the door opening even though I hadn't said yes — sheesh, no respect for privacy in the Cho household! I lifted the side of the pillow closest to the door.

"DAD!"

"I knocked," Dad said. "Breakfast is on the table."

"WHAT IF I WAS NAKED IN HERE?"

"I saw your mother give birth to you, honey; nothing will ever be as shocking as that."

Oh, gross. Now I'd have *that* image in my head all day.

"Are you okay?" Dad said, sitting on the bed like he did every night at lights-out.

I squashed the pillow back down on my head.

"This isn't like you, Chloe."

"Mummumng mime bee," I said into the mattress.

"Honey, I really can't hear you, can you take the pillow off of your head, please?"

I thought about it, then shoved the pillow to the side of the bed, trapping it between my body and the wall.

"Nothing's like me," I said.

"I don't understand what that means," Dad said. He stroked my hair with his hand, but I shook my head violently and he pulled his hand away.

"What does that even mean, *this isn't like you*? I'm not Korean, I'm not even human—everything I thought was *me* was all just made up."

Dad took a deep breath through his nose.

"It's true you're not Korean, and I'm sorry that we kept that from you for so long," he said quietly. "But it doesn't change who you are."

Yes it does.

"I'm sorry you're so upset, though. I understand."

No you don't.

Dad leaned over and kissed the back of my head.

"You still need to get up, honey. Breakfast is on the table."

He got up and walked out of my room, leaving the door wide open. Typical. I could smell bacon, though, and I realized I was actually hungry, so I only waited another ten minutes before dragging myself out of bed.

Mom and Dad were both finished eating, and Mom had all her work stuff already on her when I dragged my sorry, best-friendless carcass to the table. Mom and Dad kissed, which didn't gross me out like usual because what did it matter? What did anything matter? Let 'em suck face till the sun exploded.

"There's our sleepyhead," Mom said with a half smile. I grunted at her in response, which would normally get me a comment about manners and stuff, but this time Mom just kissed me on the cheek, whispered "I love you" into my ear, and went out the door.

I sat down at the table and stared glumly at my place mat. It was the same plastic *Rocket Cats* place mat I'd had since I was five. It was scuffed up and faded, but you could still see the Rocket Cats pretty clearly, jet packs firmly on their backs, blasting off to fight crime in Calico City. I wondered how the Rocket Cats would feel if they found out they were actually stingrays or centipedes. I'd always loved that place mat, but suddenly I felt like throwing it out the window. Dad put a plate of bacon, eggs, and toast right in the middle of the place mat, and depressed or not, I wanted the bacon, so I picked up a piece with my bare hand and took a bite.

Dad sat across from me with his favorite coffee mug, the one with the logo of the Georgia Aquarium on it, cradled in both hands.

"Something happened," he said, taking a sip.

I shrugged, finished chewing my bacon, and swallowed.

"Shelley and I had a fight."

"Oh." Dad put his mug down. "That hasn't happened very often, has it?"

I snorted.

"NOTHING that's happened lately has happened very often before, Dad."

"I'm sure you'll be able to patch it up with her."

I glared at him, suddenly feeling both depressed AND mad.

"It's your fault. You and Mom." My tone was strong enough to make Dad lean back from the table.

"Okay," he said, frowning slightly. "I don't understand, can you explain?"

"Explain what? You and Mom lied to me, like, over and over and over."

"I know, honey," Dad said with a wince. "I know you're struggling with that, I just don't understand what it has to do with Shelley. Did you . . ." His eyes opened a little wider. ". . . Did you *tell* her about it?"

I crossed my arms and let out a deep sigh.

"Yes, Dad. Mom already knows I told Shelley. She's my best friend, you know."

Was my best friend, anyway, and I dropped my slice of bacon onto my plate, tried not to start crying, and started crying anyway.

"Oh, Chloe," Dad said. He got up and came around the table, but I shoved my chair back from the table, scrambled to my feet, and backed away from him. He stopped in his tracks.

"It's YOUR FAULT!" I shouted, furiously pressing my knuckles against my eyes to try and stop crying. "She was only friends with me because I was Korean, and now I'm not and we're not friends anymore!"

"Whoa, hold on," Dad said. He held his hands straight out from his body, palms down. "I have a hard time believing Shelley feels that way."

"How would you know? She's not YOUR friend!"

Dad smiled.

"Honey, I've known you and Shelley for your entire lives. I was there when you first met each other in day care. I was there for your first playdate at Shelley's house."

I still had my hands up in a keep-off-the-Chloe gesture, so Dad looked behind him, pulled a chair out from the table, turned it around, and sat on it. He put his hands together like he was praying, and leaned forward.

"Did Shelley actually say those things?"

I slowly lowered my hands and thought about it. What exactly had Shelley said?

". . ."

"I'm sorry, honey, I can't hear you."

"No," I grumbled.

"Has she ever said those things?"

I thought about it some more.

"No."

I looked at my feet, and my whole body kind of sagged as I stood there.

"I know how hard this is for you, Chloe, and none

of it's your fault. Okay? You haven't done anything wrong, and you haven't actually changed, right?"

"It feels like it."

"You DIDN'T and you HAVEN'T," Dad said, putting some extra oomph into it. "Think about it, honey. Why are you and Shelley best friends? Why did she pick you?"

"I told you, because I'm Korean. And probably also because nobody else will hang out with her."

Dad stood up, put his hands on his hips, and put on his "Wut?" face.

"In preschool?? Do you really think Shelley had some kind of Asian fetish when she was three years old?"

It did sound kind of silly when he said it like that.

"Do you know why kids become best friends at three years old?"

"No," I grumbled.

"Because they like playing with each other," Dad said. "Which is actually not as simple as it sounds, because not every kid likes playing with every other kid. You and Shelley had a bond right from the start, and it only grew over time."

"Yeah, but the Korean thing—"

"Honey, Shelley isn't best friends with you because she's interested in your Korean ancestry. She's interested in your Korean ancestry because you're her best friend."

"But she thinks I'm someone totally different from who I am!"

"No she doesn't. No."

"So then what, Dad, are you saying where we come from doesn't have anything to do with who we are??"

Dad scrubbed his forehead with the heel of one palm.

"That's not what I'm saying. Of course it's part of who we are. But it's not why you and Shelley are friends."

"But . . ."

But what if you're wrong?

"I don't know what you girls said to each other the other night, but my guess is that Shelley feels as bad about this as you do. I know your mom and I have betrayed your trust, and I'm sorry. We have some work to do to fix that. But that's got everything to do with us, and nothing to do with Shelley."

"But I just . . . I wanted . . ."

I covered my face and sucked in a long breath through the crack between my hands.

"You wanted what?" Dad said, and his voice was super gentle, and I knew he loved me, and I was so, so sad.

"I liked being Korean," I said. "It was like . . . I knew who I was, at least kind of. And now I don't, and we don't have any family, and we can't ever visit the places you and Mom lived when you were kids, and . . . I don't get to have any of that."

Dad was silent for a minute, then walked over and slowly put his arms around me. I didn't throw my arms around him in return or anything like that, but I didn't stop him either.

"I'm so, so sorry," he finally said. "It's a huge loss, sweetie. I know it is. I'm sorry."

"Thanks," I whispered.

"I was about your age when I got my first aquarium," Dad said.

I looked up at him, startled.

"On Tau Ceti?"

"Yes. On Tau Ceti. There was a store I really liked near our home—I belonged to a club that met there every day after school. I met some of my best friends in that club."

"I wish I could see it," I said.

"I wish I could take you there," Dad said. "And I wish you could meet my old friends."

"Do you think about them a lot?"

"Every day."

"Thanks for telling me," I said.

"You're welcome."

I snuffled, wiped my nose on my sleeve, and stepped away from him.

He looked at the clock on the wall, which made me look at the clock too, and I was shocked to see it was only five minutes until the first bell at school. I was never that late, and a wild impulse to play hooky and force Dad to tell me more stories jumped into my head for just a second. Then my academic ninja training reasserted itself.

"I'm late," I said with a sniffle.

"Come on, I'll drive—you can still make it on time," Dad said.

Being driven to school wasn't unprecedented, but it was unusual enough to feel weird, especially when we got there and nobody was hanging around outside. The bell rang as I was getting out of the car, and I instinctively bolted for the door, leaving the car door open and not saying bye to Dad. I did look back as I opened the front door of the school and went in, and saw Dad with his hands pressed to his head, the car still sitting at the curb.

There were still kids in the hallways, some of them hurrying like me, others just kind of moseying along like they weren't in school at all. It was like watching a movie about the ocean where they show all the different kinds of creatures that come out at night instead of the day. I didn't even recognize everyone. It was like seeing life on another planet, har de har har. I dashed to homeroom and made it through the door just as the second bell rang.

Everybody was staring at me like I was some kind of zoo animal—and hey, maybe I was. It was weird, since at least three other kids came in right after me, and I would have just stared everyone down like usual, except for some reason I couldn't. So I put my head down and headed for my seat, moving on autopilot. Except when I got there, somebody was already sitting in it. Because I was looking down, at first I only saw the backpack on top of the desk. It took hearing Shelley's voice for me to look up.

"Sorry, that seat's taken."

I looked up. The first thing I saw was Shelley's face, looking very angry and very nervous at the same time. Then I looked at the person sitting at MY desk.

"Hi, Chloe."

It was Lindsay Crisp. My best friend, the other smartest kid in school, had replaced me with the dumbest kid in school.

TWENTY-NINE

"That's my seat, Lindsay."

"We cleared it with the teacher," Shelley said in her mad-but-scared-but-trying-not-to-show-it voice.

"Sh-Shelley said you didn't want to sit here anymore," Lindsay said, looking at me and Shelley by turning her head back and forth like a hummingbird.

Ow, OW, why did Shelley do that?? What a liar!

"Oh she did, huh?" I said, not showing how badly it hurt.

"Yeah, I did." Shelley wasn't backing down.

"So what, you two are best friends or something now?"

"Um, I don't—" Lindsay said, but I cut her off.

"Fine, who cares. You're right, I don't want to sit here."

"Fine," Shelley said.

I walked past them both without a second look, and sat in Lindsay's old seat, three seats behind Shelley. It felt wrong sitting there, not just because I wasn't sitting with Shelley, but also because every-thing was farther away, the announcements sounded different, and I could hear stuff from the back of the room that I was able to ignore before.

The bell for first period rang, which was when I realized Shelley and I were in three other classes together. Did she want to sit separately in all of them? I decided I better get there first and defend my seat — if Shelley wanted to sit separately, SHE should change seats, not me!

It turned out Shelley thought the same thing, because when I elbowed my way through the crowds to get to physics she was sitting on the opposite side of the room, again next to Lindsay Crisp.

"Hey, Chloe," Tom Wolcott said. He smiled a big, toothy, crocodile smile, and I thought about the rumors that he had a crush on me. It looked like they were true. I smiled back at Tom, not because I had a crush on him too, but because he was being nice to me, and who knew how much of that I could expect to get?

It didn't even help that Mr. Goodyear was at the top of his game that day. He showed us how levers and fulcrums work by flipping a whole series of "gremlins" (the weird-looking stuffed monsters he made out of felt and cotton) around the room, putting the fulcrum at different places under the lever. Okay, it helped a little—it's hard not to be entertained by Mr. Goodyear when he's really on.

The gremlins really hit the fan when it was time for social studies, though.

"Why not?" Shelley said to Ms. Lee. The rest of the class was still filing into the room, but I was in my seat. Shelley was standing next to her seat, on the opposite side of it from me.

"Shelley, it's much too late to change partners," Ms. Lee said with a frown. "It wouldn't be fair to force anyone else to disrupt the work they've already done together."

She looked at me, and I looked to the side and shrugged.

"I can see something happened with you two, but we can't discuss it right now."

"Okay, well, I want to talk about it after class," Shelley said.

"I'm afraid I can't today, I have a parent meeting. But I think it might be a good idea to talk after school. In the meantime, I'm sorry you two are experiencing some challenges, but you need to work it out for your-selves today—changing partners just isn't an option."

Shelley huffed out a long breath and looked around the room, scanning and then stopping to look at some-one. I struggled grimly not to look, but after a second

I gave up and looked anyway. Lindsay held out her hands in an I-can't-help-it gesture, then pointed at the seat next to her, where Allie Grossman was very deliberately not looking back at Shelley.

Shelley turned back around and stared hard at the chalkboard for a second, then dropped her backpack on her desk and sat down. Ms. Lee looked at her, then me, then Shelley again. She was still frowning as she started talking to the whole class, but dropped the frown after the first few words.

"Let's get started, people. It's a work day, and if you need my help just raise your hands. We've done a lot of work to establish your country profiles individually, so really the most important thing now is to really dig into the diplomatic relationship between your two countries and work—"

Ms. Lee flicked a glance at me and Shelley again, her frown reappearing.

"—together."

THIRTY

Shelley and I spent the whole class working together, if you define "working together" as "working separately without any idea what the other person was working on." That wasn't completely true, actually — at one point Shelley knocked a book off the top of the stack she'd pulled out of her backpack, and I instinctively looked at it when it hit the floor. It had a picture of an old white guy and the French flag on the cover, so it was obviously a book about France.

I had a book about Korean political history open in front of me, but I was only pretending to take notes. What I actually did was scribble random questions to myself.

Does looking Korean but being from another galaxy mean I'm a big faker?

Should I keep telling people I'm Korean even though I'm not?

Who cares?

Et cetera.

Ms. Lee didn't stop to help me or Shelley, which was just one more thing that made it obvious something was going on between us. At one point Ms. Lee went back to her desk, where I caught her looking at me with a crinkle in her forehead. She caught my eye and smiled, then got up when two girls behind us called out for help.

At the end of class I shot out of there like a crazed ferret, but once I was out in the hall I realized I didn't want to go to the lunchroom, but I also didn't want to pass Shelley going back in the direction of the library, so I kept going and went into the nearest bathroom.

I was just about to come out of my bathroom stall when I heard the bathroom door open again and at least two girls come in. I stopped and stayed in the stall, putting down the lid and sitting on the covered toilet so at least it would look occupied if someone, I don't know, looked under the door or something.

One of the girls was Shelley.

"Seriously, don't worry about it," she said.

"I'm not worried," said a voice I recognized as Lindsay Crisp's. Oh great, now I had to listen to the new BFFs talk smack about me. Wonderful.

"I just don't want you to be mad at me," Lindsay said. "I mean, you're not like Chloe that way, you know? She's always mad about something."

???

"No she's not."

"Well, she's mad at you now, isn't she? Did you guys have a fight or something?"

"No."

Here's the thing about being best friends with someone since you were babies: You know when they're putting on a big show so nobody will know how upset they are. Shelley was definitely upset.

"Anyway, don't worry about it," Shelley said. "I understand."

I almost sucked in a breath, but managed to clamp my hands over my mouth. Was Shelley being rejected by Lindsay? Lindsay *Crisp*? Lindsay dumber-than-a-bag-of-hammers Crisp?? I felt an unexpected glow of relief, then a totally expected burst of guilt. Why did Lindsay Crisp always make me feel guilty??

"It's just, you know, I have other friends," Lindsay said. "I don't mean it like YOU don't have any friends . . ."

"It's not a big deal," Shelley said in her it's-totally-a-big-deal voice, but of course how would Lindsay recognize that voice? She hadn't spent almost every day with Shelley since preschool. She hadn't slept over at Shelley's house a thousand times. She wasn't Shelley's best friend.

I was Shelley's best friend.

"Chloe seems . . . cool," Lindsay said, sounding like a giant faker.

"She's the best," Shelley said, and aw man, I felt a little twinge, like my Popsicle of a heart was starting to thaw.

"Is it . . . hard hanging out with her?" Lindsay asked. Sigh. That didn't sound like a promising question.

"Sometimes," Shelley said.

"I'd worry about, I don't know, *offending* her," Lindsay said, getting it right for once. "Like, do you have to bow to her parents and stuff like that?"

AAAAAAAGGGGGHHHHH . . . and then Shelley stepped up.

"That's stupid," she said, and I heard Lindsay huff out a breath of air.

"Why is that stupid??" I could almost see the expression on Lindsay's face—upside-down U of a mouth, eyebrows in an upside-down V, and a general sad panda kind of vibe.

"Because Chloe's parents are like everyone else's parents, that's why. They're just normal people."

"But they're, like, foreign and stuff, so I—"

"What are you talking about? You think Chloe is foreign?"

I could hear in Lindsay's voice that she was starting to get mad.

"She IS foreign, you know—"

"Chloe's *not* foreign, Lindsay. She was born in the exact same hospital you were born in, and she's three months older than you, which means she's lived in this country three months longer than you have. And it doesn't matter, because she'd be my best friend even if she was from another planet or something."

Good one, Shelley, I thought, trying to ignore the fast-growing lump in my throat.

"Is she your best friend?" It was Lindsay's turn to put razor blades into her voice. "Because I thought you were trying to get ME to be your new best friend."

Shelley was silent.

"If I'm so stupid, how come you're the one who's practically begging me to listen to music and work together and stuff? I mean, it was fun the first time, but it's kind of creepy that you keep asking."

Wow, so mean—who knew Lindsay Crisp had it in her? I waited for Shelley to arm her missiles and blow Lindsay out of the water, but she didn't. The only sounds that came out of her were . . . what were those sounds?

Oh no. Shelley was crying.

"Are you crying?" Lindsay sounded alarmed. "Oh, Shelley, I'm sorry, I didn't mean to make you cry!"

She actually sounded like she meant it, which was probably the only reason why I didn't wring her neck right then and there.

"I'm really sorry, Shelley, I didn't mean . . . are you okay? Are you . . ."

She's not okay. You hurt her feelings. Just like I did.

Did it matter if I was Korean, an alien, or an iguana? If my best friend was out there defending me, even though she was crying because she was alone, did any of that matter?

I stood up, opened the door to the stall, and stepped out into the bathroom. Lindsay actually jumped in surprise, but Shelley just looked over her shoulder at me with tearstains all the way down her face.

"Well, that's just perfect," she said, sniffling.

"Oh my god, Chloe, were you in there that whole time??" Lindsay screeched.

"Obviously," Shelley said, catching my eye. We almost smiled at each other.

"I can't believe you were totally eavesdropping!" Lindsay put her fists on her hips and metronomed her head back and forth between me and Shelley.

"LINDSAY." I didn't yell, I just . . . spoke with authority. With my fists clenched.

"Wh-what?" Lindsay said, reverting to her normal self.

I stared her down for a second, which made her drop her OMG body language and put her hands together in front of her.

"You don't have to bow to my mom and dad. Or me. That IS stupid."

"O-okay. Sorry?"

"Don't worry about it. Now, go away."

Lindsay got a sour look on her face and shook her head.

"You are so rude, Chloe. Fine, I'll go away and leave you two alone, I hope you're very happy being all alone together." She flounced to the door, tried to slam it, realized she couldn't slam it because it's one of those hydraulic doors that can't be slammed, and was gone.

So, it was just me and Shelley in the girls' bathroom.

"Hey," I said.

"Hey. I guess you heard that whole mess."

"Yeah."

"Lindsay's not so bad, you know," Shelley said. "I mean, she says stupid things, but she's nice, and she's actually not stupid."

"She just sounds that way sometimes, huh? Sorry, sorry, I didn't mean . . ."

Silence in a school bathroom isn't actually silent, have you ever noticed that? Those bathrooms have all kinds of noises — right then, they included the sound of my own heart, although I might have been the only person hearing that one.

"I guess I'm just sorry, period," I said.

"Yeah, you are." Shelley wiped her nose with the back of her hand, stared at her hand, then turned around and started washing it.

"I don't care if you're Korean or not, you know." She turned the water off, grabbed a paper towel from the dispenser, and dried off her hands, all without turning back around to look at me.

"I know."

"Do you?" Finally she turned around, throwing the paper towel in the general direction of the trash can.

"Yeah." I looked down at my feet.

"I mean, the Korean thing was, you know, interesting and all that, and the alien thing is also . . . interesting, but who really cares?"

"Well, I KIND OF care. It's sort of my whole life and everything."

Shelley rolled her eyes.

"That's not what I mean."

"Yeah, I know."

"How do you know?" Shelley leaned back against the sink, crossed her arms, then crossed her legs at the ankles.

I took a deep breath.

"I know because when I lost Snowball at the playground that time you gave me YOUR teddy bear to replace him. That didn't have anything to do with being Korean."

Shelley gave a little snort. "I forgot about Snowball."

"I still have her, you know. Butter, that is. Best teddy bear ever."

That got a wisp of a smile out of Shelley.

"I know because when I wanted to run away from home, you came with me without hesitating, even though we only got ten blocks away before we got scared and came back."

"Before we were brought back, you mean."

When I was seven I got really, really mad at Mom and Dad for getting me a boring old big-girl bed instead of the dragon-shaped bed I really wanted, so when crying for an hour didn't do anything I decided to head for greener, dragon-friendlier pastures. I didn't actually have pastures of any kind to run away to, but that didn't stop me from crawling out the

window after dinner with my *Aoshima Island* backpack full of stuffed animals and books, going to
Shelley's house, and telling her I needed her to run
away from home with me. Which she did.

"At least we got ice cream," Shelley said.

"Yeah, but the person at the ice cream place ruined
it by calling my dad."

"Yeah, but it really was kind of scary," Shelley
said. "Fun and scary."

"Remember when Elizabeth Smith pulled down
my shorts in soccer practice in third grade?" I said.
"You were the only one that didn't laugh, and you
ran out on the field and tried to block people's view
with your sweater. Remember?"

Shelley didn't say anything that time — she smiled,
a real smile, the old just-for-Chloe smile, and it was
suddenly hard to talk because I was starting to cry
but I kept going anyway.

"I know because it's been awful not talking to you
about anything, and I know it's my own stupid fault
for not trusting you but I miss you and I still want us
to be best friends and I'm sorry, Shelley, I'm sorry,
I'm sorry . . ."

Then I was crying for real, so I had to stop talking,
but then I felt Shelley put her arms around me and

hug me, and she was crying too so I hugged her back, and it was weird to be hugging in the bathroom but I didn't care. I didn't care. My best friend. I had my best friend back, and that was the only thing I cared about.

THIRTY-ONE

AFTER SHELLEY AND CHLOE'S AWKWARD BUT Great Bathroom Reunion it was jarring to just go to lunch like normal, and I realized I had other people to apologize to, namely Ms. Lee. I'd never, ever, ever had to apologize to a teacher before, so yeah, super awkward. Shelley walked me back to the classroom.

"The door's closed," she whispered as we got closer. "Maybe she's not there."

I sighed. "She's in there."

"Okay. Well . . ." Shelley stood there for a second and we experienced the leftover discombobulation of the previous few days.

"I'll meet you in the cafeteria," I said. "Or in orchestra."

"Okay." Shelley nodded, quickly squeezed my hand, and took off. I took a deep breath, knocked, and cracked open the door. Ms. Lee looked up from a pile of papers on her desk.

"Oh!" She put down the sheaf of papers in her

hands with a rustle and thump. "Chloe, I'm so glad to see you!"

"You . . . are?" I'd been sort of shuffling my way into the room, but I totally stopped when she said that.

"Well, yes." Ms. Lee leaned on one elbow, put the other hand on her hip, and gave me a one-sided smile. "I'm always concerned when one of my best students starts having academic difficulties. And I've had my share of problems with best friends."

I blew out a long breath.

"Things are . . . you know, still complicated."

"At home, you mean, or with Shelley?" Ms. Lee gestured at the chair next to her desk, and as I sat in it she pivoted her chair to face me directly, like she always did.

"Both, but they're better," I said, and I had a flash of sadness at the thought that I'd never be able to really, honestly talk to Ms. Lee about it. "Things are . . . different."

"I'm so glad to hear that," Ms. Lee said with a smile.

"I'm sorry about being such a terrible student lately." Holy cow, that was hard—I couldn't even look at Ms. Lee while I said it.

"You don't owe any apologies to me, Chloe—I'm honestly more concerned with your well-being than with any individual assignment. You do have some catching up to do, however, and knowing your standards, I suspect we're both going to be disappointed with your grade on the project."

"I know, I know," I said, looking at the floor. "And I'm not asking for more extra credit or anything like that—"

"I'm glad to hear that."

"—it's just, I just, I'm . . . I know I've been messing up, is all I want to say. It's not going to happen anymore."

"Well, I'm glad to hear that too. So you and Shelley . . . will be able to finish the project together?"

I managed to look up again. "Yeah. We talked, everything's okay."

As I said it, I thought maybe it was true about everything else. Mom and Dad, not being Korean, being an alien . . . maybe it would all be fine.

THIRTY-TWO

I LEARNED SOMETHING ABOUT MYSELF OVER THE next couple of weeks: Being really behind on a big school project didn't just make me mad, it also freaked me out.

"How do people who leave their work until the last minute *do* this all the time??" I dropped my pencil and rubbed my eyes with the heels of my hands. Playing catch-up with the Model UN project was bad enough all by itself, but I also had to catch up on all of my other schoolwork.

"Duh, they don't do it all the time," Shelley said. "They wait until the last minute, then try to catch up."

"That's not what I mean. How do they stand KNOWING they'll have to do all of the work at the last minute? It's so stressful!"

"Maybe they just don't think about it. Or care."

"I don't understand that at all," I grumbled.

"Me either."

"It doesn't make any sense! Doing everything at the last minute is so much harder . . ."

"Geez, Chloe, snap out of it."

"I don't get it—if you wait until the last minute you practically have to study yourself to death to have any chance at an A," I said.

"Or if you're Joel Morrissey, you just take the D instead." Shelley grinned wickedly.

I let my hands drop onto the table with a double thunk and stared at them, feeling really hopeless about school for the first time in my life.

"I can't do it," I said quietly.

"Can't do what?" Shelley said, fishing a candy bar out of her backpack and tearing it open.

"Catch up. I'm too far behind."

"No ur not," Shelley mumbled around a mouthful of chocolate and caramel. "Peesh uv cake, lesh get back to—"

I threw my pencil down on the desk hard enough to make it bounce, hit the wall, and clatter onto the floor behind the desk, with all the electrical cords and dust bunnies. I lurched out of my chair, sat on the bed next to Shelley, and flopped onto my back.

"Come on, Chloe." Shelley poked my shoulder with the eraser end of her pencil. "Miles to go before we sleep and all that."

"Oh, very good," I said in my fake British accent. "Poetry, well done."

"Geez, that accent sounds even worse than usual. Get up."

"What if . . ." I had to stop because I knew it was a stupid question.

"What if what?"

"What if doing this report is plagiarism?"

Shelley frowned at me, picked up the messy stack of books and papers on the bed, and plopped them down on my stomach.

"OOF," I said, picturing a comic book speech bubble around it in my head. "What are you—"

"You know what that pile of stuff on your stomach is?" Shelley said.

"Heavy?"

"RESEARCH, CHO! You know, that thing you do when you're NOT just copying somebody else's work?"

"Actually, we could plagiarize this stuff really easily—"

"You're not plagiarizing, so shut up and get back to work." Shelley smacked the mountain of papers with her hand, which made me go "oof" for real. I pushed the stack onto the bed without messing it up too much—that stuff has to stay in order, you know—and sat up.

"Why are you doing this?" I said, looking at Shelley with my head tilted back on my neck. That made my neck hurt, so I raised my head back up to a normal position.

"Doing what?" Shelley didn't look up from the book she'd started flipping through. "Working, like you're supposed to be doing?"

"No—well, yeah, but no. I mean, you know, helping. Me."

"You're kidding, right?" Shelley slapped a Post-it onto a page and scribbled a note on it.

"I'm not saying I've been *mean* to you or anything, but I've . . . you know . . ."

"Are you talking about how you've been totally mean to me?"

I fought off the urge to slap myself in the face. "Yeah, that."

Shelley finally closed the book and looked at me. She reached behind me, grabbed my pillow (I had to stop myself from tumbling backward), tucked it behind her, and leaned back. This time she stared straight at the wall on the opposite side of the room, where my Tiger Rabbit poster was before I tore it down. I missed my Tiger Rabbit poster.

"Do you remember Jill Hardy's birthday party in third grade?" Shelley said.

"Uhhh . . . kind of. Oh, right, yeah. The dress."

Shelley fiddled with the knobs on her watch, twisting her wrist back and forth.

"Right, the dress."

"They weren't even all that pretty," I said. "The collars were stupid."

"I LIKED that dress," Shelley said, looking at me with her head tilted sideways, and I wanted to hear what she had to say, so I clamped both hands over my mouth.

"That's better." Shelley stared me down for a second longer—just making sure, I guess—then leaned her head back against the wall.

"My POINT is, Jill liked the dress too, which made sense since she was the one wearing it, and when she spilled grape juice on it and blamed me, which made her mom yell at me too, everyone sat there and watched except you."

I smiled at the memory. "You know, I didn't care that we weren't ever allowed to go back there. And it was worth being grounded just to see the look on Mrs. Hardy's dumb face."

Shelley turned her head and looked at me—she wasn't smiling, but she didn't have her scary zombie face on either. "She was so not used to kids yelling back at her. You *yelled at somebody's mom* for me."

I looked back at Shelley and smiled. It was a slow, broken-feeling smile, like only some parts of my face were working right. "Well, duh, yeah."

"Remember when you taught me how to make origami frogs?"

"I just demonstrated it; you figured the rest out yourself."

"No, you taught me. I didn't tell you because I didn't want you getting all conceited about it." Shelley's smile got a little bigger as she said that, and a tiny ball of warmth came to life inside my chest.

"Your mom was so mad," I said, remembering the paper scraps all over the floor of Shelley's living room. "We made a lot of those frogs."

"HUNDREDS of frogs," Shelley said. "Mom actually found some in the refrigerator."

We giggled at the same time, and I suddenly realized how much I missed that.

Shelley turned away and looked at the empty spot on the wall again.

"You totally kept me from losing it when my dad got sick," she said in a quiet voice. "My mom was so out of it, remember?"

I did remember. The winter Shelley's dad had open-heart surgery was the worst. Shelley spent a lot of time crying. I went to the hospital once with Mom and Dad, and it was scary seeing Mr. Drake with all those tubes coming out of him like that.

"It was fun having you stay over here so much," I said.

"Yeah, it was. I mean, no, my dad being in the hospital wasn't fun, but you know what I mean."

"Yeah, I know."

"You're my best friend," Shelley said. "I don't care if you're Korean or if you're from a planet in the Oort cloud or whatever."

"The Oort cloud's too cold to support life," I said, sounding a little croaky because of the lump that was forming in my throat.

"Oh, look who's the big Oort cloud expert just because she's an ALIEN now."

I snort-laughed.

"It would be cool if you guys had a spaceship in a secret cave under your garage, though."

"Under the greenhouse would be better," I said. "You know, so the ship's advanced technology could be used to secretly maintain the glow-in-the-dark fish habitat."

"Ooh, maybe we should—"

"Too late, I already looked. No secret doors."

We giggled, and then I sighed.

"Making Korean food was fun," I said.

"We can still do it, can't we?"

"Yeah, but it won't be the same. It'll be . . . it won't be real the way it was before."

"I guess not. I bet you it'll still be fun, though. As long as we do it together, anyway. And your dad won't have to lie to us about how his mom made it exactly the same way back in Korea, right?"

"Right."

"You're my best friend. I'm *your* best friend. DEAL with it, Cho."

"Didn't we just have this conversation?" I said.

"It's a good conversation. I don't mind having it again."

Shelley stood up, looked down at me, and held out her hand. I looked at it for a second, then put my non-Korean, space alien hand in it. Shelley grinned, a toothy, fierce, radiant grin.

"I'm helping you, not doing it for you," she said. "Got it?"

I grinned back. "Got it."

Shelley nodded, then pulled me to my feet.

"Let's get to work."

THIRTY-THREE

IN THE LATEST CHAPTER OF *CHLOE CHO'S Adventures in New, Humiliating Experiences in Life*, the day of our final Model UN presentation arrived way too fast. Shelley and I worked our butts off—I had, like, no butt left from doing so much work—but we just ran out of time, so when we walked into class that day I felt a totally unfamiliar mix of embarrassment and fear.

"We're so screwed," I said as we took our seats at the front of the class. I felt like a giant spotlight was on me up there, and I wondered if that was the feeling that made the burnouts and losers sit in the back of the room. It was new to me. Ironic hooray, another new experience!

"Yeah," Shelley said. "But at least we're not F-minus screwed, you know?"

"How do you know?"

"Because we actually have something to present.

You can't get an F if you can prove you actually tried to do some work, and our crappy project is proof."

Gee whiz, that was comforting. I sank down in my chair.

"Welcome to the first annual Model United Nations summit!" Ms. Lee said with a big smile. "I want to thank everyone for all the hard work you've done over the past few weeks—I know it's been demanding, but you've done some fantastic work. I'm proud of you. Let's get started!"

As usual, the quality of the presentations was all over the map. Eric Flynn and Bill Castle made their entire project about sports, although they had to focus on soccer since they don't play American football in Portugal and Switzerland. Lindsay Crisp was maybe a little too obvious about not looking at me or Shelley, but it was probably hard since we were literally six feet away from her during her whole presentation, and she and Allie Grossman actually did a decent project on India and Pakistan. I couldn't decide between cutting Lindsay some slack for not being as dumb as I liked to say she was and throttling her for being mean to Shelley, but then it was our turn to present.

We got up there in front of the class with no video

or sound, no props, not even any paper handouts. It was the least prepared I'd ever been for a project. It was the only time I'd ever been anything less than 125 percent prepared for a project! I gulped, wishing for a glass of water, and looked at Shelley. She looked back, totally confident, happy, not at all worried. My best friend. I relaxed a little bit.

"I am Christine de Talleyrand-Périgord, senior diplomat from France," Shelley announced.

"I am Kyung-Wha Chung, senior diplomat from South Korea," I said in almost my normal presenting-in-class voice.

We made it through all the way to the end. We talked, and talked some more, and read some stuff that we'd written and printed out, and it was okay. It was definitely the worst project I'd ever done in school, and I felt some creeping guilt that it was also the worst project Shelley had ever done in school, but it wasn't the worst project ANYONE had ever done in school. It wasn't even the worst project anyone did that day.

At the end of our presentation the class applauded. It was nice, polite applause, nothing like the shrieking and jumping around at a Tiger Rabbit concert. But no spitballs were fired, nobody booed, and some people even clapped like they meant it. Ms. Lee nodded and clapped too, although she didn't look totally thrilled like she did when Joel Morrissey and Robbie Schumacher whipped out their 3-D animation showing the intensely messed-up history between Iraq and Kuwait. It had maybe five pieces of actual information in it, but it looked cool, and it seemed like they might actually be good at the animation thing, which was new. Robbie Schumacher's only visible skill before then was being a bully, so yay, I guess.

So unfair that exceeding the teacher's low expectations got such a HOORAY reaction, but whatever. Life's unfair, right?

THIRTY-FOUR

Ms. Lee gave Shelley and me a B- on our final Model UN presentation, and unlike my previous B-, I actually thought it was a fair grade. Not a FUN grade, but a fair one. We still needed something to wash the nasty B- taste out of our mouths, though, which was why it was perfect when Primrose Heights Public Library announced its first annual Graphic Novel Making Contest. Shelley and I had the *perfect* idea, and we started spending every Saturday afternoon working on it.

"MOOOOOOM! DAAAAAAAD! Do you know where my library card is?" I yelled as I swept my arm back and forth under the living room couch. There was all kinds of crap under there, but nothing that felt like a library card.

"Probably wherever you left it last time," Dad said from the other side of the house, where he was repairing the toaster oven's hyperdrive engine or something.

"Oh, har de har har, Dad. So funny. Hey, can I use yours?"

"Nope."

"Aw come on, Dad, it's for our graphic novel project!"

"Nope. I can't go to the library right now, and part of the responsibility of having a library card is—"

"Keeping track of where it is, blah blah, yeah, I know. MOM, CAN I—"

"Don't ask me," Mom said. At least that's what I think she said. Her voice was even more muffled than Dad's—she was probably digging around in the closet.

"Look under the couch," Dad said, briefly appearing in the hallway, then disappearing again.

"I just did! Gah! Where is it?" I said, scratching my head.

"Let's just use mine," Shelley said for the third time. She was sitting on the couch I'd just looked under and scribbling intently in a notepad.

"Check out books with YOUR card?" I gave her a look of horror that wasn't entirely fake. "I'd only be able to get half as many books!"

"Oh, I wouldn't let you use half of my limit," Shelley said with a grin. "But you could totally check out, say, ten books."

"Do you know how long it'd take me to read ten graphic novels?"

"Two weeks?"

"Oh, you're so funny. I—hey, wait." I'd stuffed my hands into the back pockets of my jeans as we were talking, and I slowly pulled my right hand out, holding my library card.

Shelley did a miniclap in front of her chin.

"Wow, it's amazing that you found it!" she said in a superfake tone of surprise.

"Oh, shut up and let's just go," I grumbled.

Dad walked into the living room with a lightbulb in one hand and a screwdriver in the other.

"Oh hey, Mr. Cho, thanks for all of your help with the biology stuff," Shelley said. "It's so weird that the oceans on TC4 were so much like the oceans here."

"You're very welcome," Dad said, replacing the burned-out bulb in the floor lamp. "It was one of the reasons we chose this planet."

Would I ever get used to Mom and Dad just talking about their lives on Tau Ceti Four like that? So weird. Great, but weird.

"We're totally gonna win," I said. "We'll have the only space alien graphic novel that's based on a true story."

"Your confidence is very reassuring," Dad said.

"Hey, it's not bragging if it's true."

"Can you girls do me a favor and get the mail before you leave?" Dad said as he headed for the kitchen.

"Sure," I said. "Come on, Shelley."

I grabbed Shelley by the elbow and pretty much dragged her down the front walk to the mailbox. It was stuffed with the usual pile of crap for Mom and Dad—lame magazines, bills, catalogs for places that sold dishes—but there was also an envelope with my name on it. It was from GeneGenie.

"I thought you didn't send them another sample!" Shelley said as I held the envelope out so she could see the GeneGenie logo on it.

"I didn't." I stuck the pile of mail under my arm, dropping half of it on the ground in the process, and opened the envelope. "Maybe they decided I'm human after all."

"Or maybe they found something new?"

Shelley leaned her head against mine as I read the letter inside. It was short and sweet, just three lines long. But they were three amazing lines, especially the first one.

Shelley and I looked at each other—her big, hazel, white-person eyes were open as wide as my brown, pseudo-Korean eyes.

"Does that mean what I think it means?" she said in a hushed voice.

"I think it does." I gulped, then grabbed Shelley's elbows and stood there trembling as it sank in.

"Are you gonna tell your folks?" she said.

"Right now," I said in a wobbly voice. We locked eyes, squealed in excitement, jumped a couple of times, then finally let go of each other.

"I should probably, you know, tell them in private," I said in a quiet voice.

"Well, duh," Shelley said with a huge grin. "What if I just meet you at the library? I can probably read at least twenty graphic novels by the time you get there."

"Oh, you wish."

There was a minute of silence then, because the old butterflies filled up my stomach again, plus that new butterfly. The sad, I'm-not-Korean-anymore butterfly that felt like it might be a permanent addition. I hoped not, though. Not a fan of the sad butterflies.

"It's gonna be okay, Chloe," Shelley said, gently shaking me by the shoulders.

"I know, I know."

"I want to know EVERYTHING."

"I'll let you know exactly what they say!"

"You better," Shelley said, just before we wrapped our arms around each other for a hug that was so hard it almost hurt. We let go of each other, and I watched as she turned and ran in the direction of the library, obviously too excited to just walk.

My best friend, forever and ever.

I burst into the living room just as Mom emerged from the bedroom in her yoga clothes.

"Well now, *someone's* excited," she said with a smile as I shoved the unimportant mail into her hands. "The graphic novel project must be going well!"

"It's going super well," I said. "Our drawings of Tau Ceti aren't nearly as good as yours, though. Mom, I—"

"Oh, thank you, honey," Mom said, twisting her hair up into a ponytail. "But I can't—"

"Forget about that! Mom, you have to look at this," I said, waving the GeneGenie.com letter over my head. "You're not gonna BELIEVE this."

"Chloe, did you get the mail—oh, I see, thank you!" Dad said as he reentered the living room. He gave Mom a really long, long hug and an equally long kiss. So rude to make me wait like that. Also, ew.

"Nice outfit," he said. Mom laughed, then brought Dad's hand to her lips and kissed it.

"Augh, I have something to show you guys!" I said, ignoring all the gross kissing and stuff and pulling on each of their sleeves.

"What, what, what?" Dad said as I grabbed his arm, grabbed Mom's arm, and pulled them both right up next to each other. I looked at the letter, found the right paragraph, stuck my fingertip on it, then held it up for them to see.

"THIS."

> *Congratulations! Your GeneGenie profile has found 1 match.*
>
> *Mitochondrial Sequence Compatibility: 100%*
> *Location: South Korea*

Mom and Dad stared at the paper in silence. I held it in front of their faces for a few seconds, then clapped it against my chest with both hands and grinned at them, bobbing up and down.

"What . . . is this, Chloe?" Mom said.

"It's a genealogy test! You know, one of those DNA things?"

"Yes, I know what those are, but what is THIS? Is this from your DNA sample?"

I sighed and let my arms flop down to my sides.

"No, Mom, I sent in a python DNA sample. YES, IT'S MINE."

They looked at each other with serious deer-in-the-headlights expressions on their faces, but then Mom gulped, and Dad quickly ran his hands through his hair a couple of times.

"You don't think—" Dad said.

"I was the best astrophysics student there, but I wasn't the only one," Mom said. She rubbed her temples with the heels of her palms.

"It's someone from TC4, isn't it? Someone else got away!" I said.

"There's no way to know," Mom said. "Unless . . ."

I'd never seen that expression on Dad's face before—it was like he was feeling ALL of the feelings all at the same time, and his face could barely hold them all without bursting into flames.

"Unless," he said, and smiled. Then they both looked at me, and for a second they had the old Operation-Keep-Chloe-in-the-Dark look on their faces, but then their faces changed. Mom looked . . . excited?

Yes, excited. So did Dad. They were both looking at me, REALLY looking at me, with big, big smiles, and OH MY GOD I WAS SO EXCITED.

"Is it a friend of yours? A family member?? WHO IS IT?"

Mom laughed, a real throw-your-head-back-and-laugh-up-at-the-sky laugh. Dad took a deep, deep breath, put his forehead against mine, then grabbed me and Mom in a crushing bear hug. When he spoke, his voice was like an entire orchestra hitting a crescendo.

"Let's find out."

Acknowledgments

I go on and on about Arthur Levine, but he's a genius editor and a beloved friend, so what, you expect me to lob decomposing tomatoes at him? I also make a lot of jokes about Send Your Agent a Neurotic Email Day (news flash: not a real holiday), but I should really talk about Ammi-Joan Paquette Is All Kinds of Fabulous Day, because she truly is. I'm not stopping with the neurotic emails, though, SORRY, JOAN.

Thank you to my bandmates in Erin Murphy's Dog: Ruth Barshaw, Arthur Levine, Jeannie Mobley, Kristin Nitz, Deborah Underwood, Carrie Watson, and Conrad Wesselhoeft. The Dawgs lift my spirits when they're at a low ebb, shout to the rafters when I have reason to celebrate, and help me park my hindquarters in the chair and do the real work. On a related note, I've moved past humblebragging and on to plain old bragging about being a client of the Erin Murphy Literary Agency, which is jam-packed with people I both respect and adore.

My friends and colleagues on the We Need Diverse Books team are breathtakingly intelligent, supremely articulate, and powerful beyond measure. The work we do together gives meaning to my career on a level it previously lacked.

You know who's awesome? The team at Arthur A. Levine

Books/Scholastic: Antonio Gonzalez, Tracy van Straaten, Lizette Serrano, Emily Heddleson, Saraciea Fennell, Weslie Turner, Emily Clement, Carol Ly, Phil Falco, Kait Feldmann, Roz Hilden, Nikki Mutch, Elizabeth Krych, Annie McDonnell, Bess Braswell, Michael Strouse, and everyone I'm leaving out but planning to treat to a doughnut if they're willing to meet me at Donut Savant in Oakland.

Nick Thomas and Eunice Kim are no longer with AAL, but I won't forget their contributions to making *U.S.O.* a reality. The good people of Paper Dog Studio created a fabulous, evocative cover. Working with Kirsten Cappy and Curious City has been a big, glitter-coated, unicorn-shaped basket of good times. Thanks to Wendy Buck at Ancestry.com, who answered my very silly questions with cheerful professionalism, and Dr. Anthony Ferrante of Columbia University, who contributed a high-octane dose of scientific knowledge.

Last but not least are Miranda, Zoe, and Leo, my family. What do you say about the people who mean more to you than anyone else ever has or ever will? What do you say to the people who made your other, even bigger dreams come true just by existing? Kudos? Let's go to In-N-Out Burger? Oh, I know: I love you.

MIKE JUNG is the author of *Geeks, Girls, and Secret Identities* and contributed to the anthologies *Dear Teen Me*, *Break These Rules*, and *59 Reasons to Write*. He is a library professional by day, a writer by night, and a semi-competent ukulele player during all the times in between. Mike is proud to be a founding member of the #WeNeedDiverseBooks team. He lives in Oakland, California, with his wife and two young children.